MW01205761

GHOST REVELATIONS

THE GHOST DUD SERIES

ASPEN BLACK

Copyright © 2019 Aspen Black

All rights reserved. This book or any portion thereof may not be reproduced or used in any manner whatsoever without the express written permission of the publisher except for the use of brief quotations in a book review.

Any references to historical events, real people, or real places are used fictitiously. Names, characters, and places are products of the author's imagination.

Front cover image by Zoe Perdita

Book design by Zoe Perdita @Rainbow Danger Designs.

Facebook: Aspen Black -Author

Facebook Group: Aspen Black and Adammeh's Wanderers

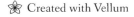 Created with Vellum

ACKNOWLEDGMENTS

I never read the acknowledgements page when I would read a book. It wasn't until I started to write again, that I realized how much work is done and why this page is here.

I want to thank everyone who encouraged me in writing this book. It's been in my mind playing around for a few years. I used to write in school, but adulting happened, I lost my love of it. It wasn't until earlier this year, 2019, that I decided to pick it up again. I have not looked back since.

Thank you to my friends and family who encouraged me. A big shout out to Jessica, Devon, Nick, Heather, and Jacob. I know I am like a rabbit when I get excited and can get a little annoying. Thanks for sticking with me!

Jessica, thanks for your hard work, I know it was a time crunch! Adammeh, you were my rock through this all.

You have been the best friend anyone would be jealous to have. Thank you for the artwork in this book.

I hope you love this book as much as I do.

Come join me on my Facebook group or Twitter account for updates, previews, and just a lot of fun!

CHAPTER 1

*W*hen they said that beauty is in the eye of the beholder, they had obviously never met Carl. The nasty gnome was a whole three feet and four inches of mean. Most gnomes were social and had manners. Not Carl. It was like his mother had dropped him on his head and punt kicked him out the door just to get away from him.

"Look, blondie," the gnome drawled like he was the Gods' gift, "I want a gin and tonic on my tab. Just like last time."

"Well, ugly, unlike last time," I leaned forward, placing my hands on the bar, "you don't have any proof of money for a tab." Not to mention he was a horrible tipper. No matter how many times he came in over the years, he never tipped more than two or three dollars when his bill was in the hundreds. And another thing, I wasn't even blonde! "And after your check bounced in 1997 you know Ray only takes cash or card from you."

Carl growled, showing off a mouth full of grey, flesh rendering teeth. Add in his rank breath and it was almost vomit inducing.

"Either give me something as collateral or a credit card." I wasn't backing down. Guys like Carl never took no for an answer. You had to put your foot down or they would walk all over you.

"Come on, Vickie," we had now graduated to begging which wasn't an improvement, "Just one drink! I am dying here!"

"No. Money first or no drink, " and just as he looked like he was about to leap over the bar, "and if you don't like it, you can bring it up with Akira."

The mention of the bar's bouncer and all-around handyman gave Carl pause. Akira was second in command of the local werewolf pack and was dangerous dipped in strawberry syrup. He was a sexy and dangerous wolf most people with a brain didn't cause trouble with. He was also one of my best friends and did I mention the part where he's dessert lickable worthy? I might have a small crush on the second in command.

"I'll remember this, Vickie. Mark my words!" I just shook my head at him. His short body combined with his disproportionately large hands and round gnome nose was not anything someone would be intimidated by, even with the teeth. Carl slid off the bar stool with a thump and, while shaking the middle finger at me, walked to the door and out into the damp and muggy afternoon.

Ah, monsoon season. Don't let anyone fool you with, 'Arizona is a dry heat.' That's a bunch of horse shit. Monsoon season was usually only during early summer but this year it decided to be a pain and stick around longer.

"I'll rue the day, yada yada yada." Grumbling, I grabbed the rag and continued to wipe the counter. At least this time there was no furniture damage. Uncle Ray got grumpy when he had to replace furniture in the bar. It got expensive, especially where the supernatural community was involved.

Supes Karaoke Bar was a popular destination for the supernatural in the great city of Gilbert, Arizona. It was a standalone building on a corner not far from the main street of town. If a human tried to enter, a ward encouraged them to go home and sleep. The bar was frequented by the things that go boo in the dark and had been in service for a little over eighty years.

It had been my home away from home ever since I could walk. I touched the carved 'V was here' in the far corner of the bar top and smiled. I had done this when I was twelve and Uncle Ray had been so mad until I had started to cry. That was the one thing that almost always made the alpha werewolf panic. He still grumbled about the carving even now all the while wiping it clean and making sure it shone like a trophy.

A jingle rang out behind me, signaling someone coming out of the back room. A glance over to the right showed Akira walking out from the back carrying two boxes of miscellaneous bottled alcohol. Those boxes weighed close to fifty pounds each and he just carried them with one arm. Show off.

I was banned from trying to bring inventory to the front. The last time I had brought out a case, I ended up dropping it and that particular case of wine had cost a pretty penny. In my defense, it had been a heavy case, the lighting was terrible, and a ghost had popped half its body up through the case to say hello.

Yup, I can see, and converse, with ghosts. Out of all the magical beings in my family, I was what my mother considered a dud. No powers except the ghosts. Freaked out my mom for a while. Seeing ghosts was weird to her even though she is a powerful grey witch. Most of the community laughed at it. Seeing and talking to ghosts was for humans who like to play. Uncle Ray was the only one in my family who seemed to have any interest in them. He liked to hear the stories, especially when he was halfway through a case of whiskey.

"Hey Vic, having any trouble? I heard some raised voices from the freezer." Akira's gentle voice was easily my favorite thing in the world. He could curl your toes with his slow drawl. Akira was a lone wolf born in Texas before moving to Arizona at the age of twenty-two. Akira had strolled through the doors of the bar as if he didn't have a care in the world.

He was easily seven feet tall; his shoulder-length hair was as black as onyx and tipped with red. He made you think of a dashing rogue who would steal your heart. His almond-shaped eyes were silver with flecks of blue were just the icing on top. Every time he was near me, I felt safe and warmth always flooded my body.

"Nah. Carl was here but I sent him off. He was just pmsing." I grinned at him throwing the cleaning rag over my left shoulder. "Can I help?"

A loud snort was my answer. I threw the rag at him as he set the cases down on the just cleaned bar.

"You know the rules. You don't get to touch any alcohol until it's out of the cases and on the bar." A flash of teeth in a hallmark smile with a right dimple caused my stomach to flutter like it always did.

"Drop a single case worth thousands of dollars one time." I scoffed and started putting away the bottles of various brands as he handed them to me. "Are you excited for the summer solstice party tonight?" We were overstocking the bar for tonight. Cook had been slaving away preparing the food most of the afternoon.

It was a long-standing tradition for Uncle Ray's bar to throw a party late in the night after most had finished their summer solstice ceremonies. Most shifters didn't care about the day itself, but any excuse to party, eat, drink, and dance, they were all in. It also did a service to the community as a whole. Every being was welcomed and encouraged to come, relax, and enjoy themselves. There were always one or two fights, but Uncle Ray or one of his wolves would usually break it up by tossing the offenders out on their butts.

I loved the party. It was the one night of the year every supernatural was free to be themselves. I had met my other best friend, Lola, at this party five years ago.

After a break from singing karaoke all night, she had ordered a frizzy lemonade with a shot of vodka from me. She was new to the city, having transferred from her hometown in New York as a paralegal at a supernatural law firm. If you haven't met many pixies, she would probably be the most memorable.

Pixies were often described as tricksters, happy go lucky individuals, and all around cute. That's not how you would describe Lola. Sure, she had the cute going on, but everything else? She was usually the most serious person in the room (except when she was singing Elton John) and her favorite color to wear was black.

We became fast friends that night. She had helped me kick an unruly kappa out of the bar who had been trying to mate with the water fountain near the restrooms. There had only been one hiccup in our friendship thus far. She had dated Akira for a few months without knowing I was in love with him. They had been pretty hot and heavy, but one night I snapped at both of them about getting a room and getting the hell out of my bar. It hadn't taken Lola long to corner me after and get me to fess up.

The tears were gross and the sobbing tears were worse. We did both. And a little scream crying too. Lola broke up with him the next day even though I had told her not to. I didn't want to stand in the way of either of their happiness. She'd looked at me like I was an idiot and said, "Bros before Hoes. Even though I enjoy mounting him like he's Everest and I'm the pole flag, you are more important to me." I had to try hard to keep that image out of my head for days. She even showed me some racy pictures of him I just couldn't help but look at, even though I knew it was wrong. That man is just a yumsicle topped with cream.

"I don't know," Akira's voice interrupted my musing. "It's the same every year. Everyone gets drunk and dances around like idiots." His grin gave away how much he really did enjoy the party.

"You being the one leading the drunks." An echoed grin back at him had us both laughing. "You usually drink everyone under the table and end up winning every bet."

"I wouldn't be a very good second if I let just anyone out drink me." Akira finished putting the bottles away and leaned his hip against the bar. "I hear you have a date afterwards?"

Heat flushed my cheeks as I looked down. "That was a, um, fib. So I wouldn't have to go to mom and dad's after the shift." I looked at him from the corner of my eye. "I didn't want to run into Jacob. You know how he is."

And he did. We all loved my younger brother, but he was a jackass to anyone who he deemed wasn't on the same magical level as he was. He was the golden child, the perfect mix of shifter and witch. The first and only one, as far as anyone knew. It has been nearly impossible for the different races to mix and have children that had both aspects of the parents. I was a dud but Jacob ended up perfect.

"Ah. He's back on break from school already." Akira picked up a glass, set it in front of me and picked up the soda gun, filling the glass with lemon lime soda. "Your mom is probably happy about it and wanted to have the family dinner?"

"Yup, hence the 'date' lie." I picked the glass up, sipping the soda. "Thank you, Akira. What are your plans? Want to be my date?"

"Not sure. I'll probably just help with the cleanup and head home." He reached his arms above his head stretching as he pulled one arm back by the elbow, his shirt rode up giving a peak of his smooth abs. "Although, I wouldn't be opposed to some company." His tone was sly, almost seductive, as he caught me ogling his goods, making a smirk form on his lips. "I wouldn't be opposed to being your date if it came with perks."

Our flirting had started to increase in fever lately. I mean, we flirted constantly but it had always been light and harmless. Sometimes there were flashes of heat on my side, when I would almost launch myself at him, but I always held back. It was kind of our thing, but lately it had seemed to be...more. I wasn't quite sure how to respond so it was times like these that Lola always said to wing it.

"Oh?" I put a little purr into my voice. "I could think of a few things." I stepped forward so we were only a few inches apart and placed a hand over his heart and tipped my face up.

A flash of surprise followed by heat filled his eyes. I could feel the rumble in his chest that sent a pleasant shiver through me. He pushed forward so our faces were close. Close enough to rock forward and our lips would touch. His hand touched my cheek and electricity spreads within my body and his nose flared as he sensed my desire was real and not just teasing.

His other hand covered my hand on his chest and his voice was low. "Vickie," his lips are just a breath away, "are you..."

That's when the front door banged open and we jumped apart, both of us breathing a little more rapidly than normal. My face flooded bright red and I had to clear my throat.

"Welcome to Supes Karaoke Bar! What can I get for you?" I had to struggle for a few moments to form my greeting for the two fairies flew in. "I have some cotton candy syrup laced with rum as the days special."

Akira moved past me, his back brushing mine, sending those tingly sensations down again. "We'll talk about this after the party and we've cleaned up." He disappeared into the back leaving me frustrated and more hopeful than I had been in a long time. Would we go past the friend zone finally?

CHAPTER 2

The party was just winding down a little after four in the morning. I hadn't gotten to talk to Akira much because he was with the pack, making sure everyone was behaving. Lola had made an appearance for a few minutes before going home, but she had said she wasn't feeling well, and to be honest, she didn't look well either. I promised to check in with her tomorrow. I hadn't gotten the chance to speak with her about my encounter with Akira.

"Last call!" I yelled out to the party goers as the round of applause died down after a loudly off-key version of Turn Me On by David Guetta and Nicki Minaj had concluded by a pair of brownies. It had sounded like nails on a chalkboard to me but everyone else seemed to have enjoyed it immensely. Most likely it was because almost all of them were so drunk they couldn't feel their faces.

Uncle Ray was near the door helping some more of the drunker customers outside to their ride shares. Yes, supernatural beings used Uber and Lyft just like everyone else. Would you want a drunk fae driving a Porsche into a tree or a drunk ogre dropping his pants to pee in the middle of the street because he doesn't have the sense to wait until he's home? I wouldn't.

It didn't take long after last call before the bar was nearly empty except for the pack and myself. My eyes met the gorgeous silver Akira's for a brief moment. His held a promise that left me shaking down to my toes and I bit my lower lip. This was really happening.

"Vickie," Uncle Ray's voice from beside me jerked me out of my fantasy. He wasn't a tall man. More wide than tall but that width was all muscle. He had one of those villian-esque curling mustaches as his pride and joy.I always loved to tug on it. "I'll finish cleaning up with the pack, love. You can head out."

I hadn't expected that. There was still the matter of speaking with Akira. If I left, that conversation would be put off again. I had to come up with something so I could stay and not get questioned about it.

"Ok, Uncle Ray. Can I hang around until you're done? Akira is my ride tonight." My voice squeaked slightly, but it was the first thing that came to my mind.

Uncle Ray's eyes narrowed when my voice went higher, but he didn't say anything other than, "Alright, that's fine. Go sit down and let us clean up so we can all get out of here."

My shoulders slumped in relief as he walked off. I could only imagine what he would do or say if he knew Akira and I were going to talk about 'us'. I went outside, ignoring the blast of hot muggy air. It was dark and quiet, which only happens in the early mornings for a few hours. I loved the entrance to the bar since it was off the street and the pavers that led up to the bar were worn and old. The lights on the outside were old fashioned and hadn't been changed since the three story buildings around had been built.

In an hour, the streets would start filling with people on their way to work. I looked up into the night sky, releasing a heavy sigh. Tonight had been more than I had expected. I pressed a hand over my heart as it thudded against my chest.

It wasn't just about sex, not saying sex wasn't important because I wanted him with all of my being. Akira was smart, funny, and I always felt safe with him. There were few of the male persuasion that

I enjoyed being around because of my past. I couldn't count the hours we spent together over the years. We played video games on the weekends and he helped me with my homework when I was in school. It was the little things that made my feelings for him blossom.

I had started to giggle thinking about how he punched my ex-boyfriend, Shax, when the door to the bar opened and Akira stepped outside. He saw me and walked over, leaning an arm on the wall above my head.

"So, I'm your ride for the night?" Oh, how he made that sound dirty, obviously on purpose to throw me off. His eyes glinted with amusement. "You haven't even bought me dinner yet."

I laughed leaning against the wall. "You're such a dork."

"So you've told me," he growled and pressed closer. "shall we discuss what happened earlier?"

I stared up into his face, tracing the curves of his sharp cheek-bones, the dimple on the right side, and his eyes that left me breathless.

"I have a confession." My voice was barely a whisper but that wouldn't stop his superior hearing. His head tilted slightly as I looked back down to the ground. "I've been in lo..." His index finger touched my lips, silencing my confession.

"That's not fair." He glanced around as if looking for watchers. "You can't tell me that when we are outside of your uncle's bar. Let's go somewhere less open and talk." He stepped back from me and the heat from his body disappeared. I felt cold even though it was almost a hundred degrees already.

What did he mean that it wasn't fair? If he was going to say no to my confession wouldn't it just be easier on both of us to get it over with now?

"Akira, if you don't feel the same way, just tell me." I wiped the tears that were forming furiously. "Just tell me you don't want me."

He blinked. "What? No, Vic, that's not why I want to go some-where more private." He huffed and suddenly I was in his arms. "I just wanted to do this without having to watch out for your Uncle."

And then his mouth was on mine. That electricity that had been playfully stroking my body when we touched before was now a full blown raging storm. There weren't stars. No, this was more. I didn't need air when he was kissing me.

His tongue dominated against mine as a whimper escaped between the heated and wet kisses. My back was pushed into the wall as his body pressed closer and I could feel his length hardening against me. I wanted him inside of me now. I didn't care if we were outside and anyone could see us.

That thought jerked me back. I did care, especially if it was my uncle who saw us. "Akira," gasping as I pulled away for air, "wait, what if Uncle Ray comes out?" It hurt to even stop now that I had finally had a taste of him, but I could only imagine what would happen if Uncle Ray found us outside making out like a couple of horny teenagers.

Akira's lips moved from my mouth, down my jaw, and his breath was hot as it teased my neck. He bit down on my neck pulling a cry from me as more heat pooled between my legs.

"I told you we needed to go somewhere else." He chuckled softly, sucking on my neck before pulling back. "Next time, listen to me." That's when my legs decided to give out and he had to hold me up, which seemed to amuse him even more. "Let's go to your place and talk about this."

"Talk?" I raised an eyebrow up at him. "Is that what you call what we were just doing?"

There was that smirk again. I swear his dimple would make anyone swoon. "No," he stepped back after making sure I wasn't about to faceplant into the concrete, "that was kissing you senseless. We do need to talk."

I smoothed my shirt from where it had bunched up. "Right. Talk. I guess we need to."

Akira held his hand out to me and as I took it an earth shattering scream rang out from down the block. It was loud, piercing, and the screamer was obviously terrified before it was abruptly cut off with what sounded like someone choking on water.

"Stay here, Vickie. Go inside and get Ray." Akira's face had turned serious and his features sharpened as he prepared to shift if needed. He started running to where the scream had come from.

I wasn't going to let him go alone, but I slammed the door to the bar open and cried out, "Uncle Ray! Something's happened!" With that I took off after Akira knowing my Uncle and whatever pack members remained in the bar would be right behind.

Akira had already gone around the corner and was standing in front of the laundry coin shop looking grim. There weren't any people or traffic about yet, thank goodness. I reached his side just as Uncle Ray and a few of his pack arrived on the other side of him. I looked around for the source of the scream and bit back a gasp.

A woman lay on the ground, her arms and legs spread out. She wore a simple dress that I had seen many of the witches wear earlier tonight. She wasn't wearing any shoes; one was near her head while the other was nowhere in sight. Her hair was spread about her head in a halo, like a bad joke. Her dress hadn't always been red, it had been white based on some areas of the dress, but her blood had seeped around her and the dress had become saturated in it. Her hands were curled in a claw like grip, as if she had been fighting someone.

That choking sound that we had heard earlier was explained as I got a look at her neck. Or at least, what used to be her neck. Her throat had been ripped apart, her spinal cord could be seen through the blood and ragged muscle. Even if she was a witch, there would be no way she could survive that.

Uncle Ray let out a low whistle. "Shit." He made a sharp gesture. "Secure the area. We don't want any humans to see this. Chase, call the MEPA." As Uncle Ray was giving out his orders, I approached the woman's body when I noticed her chest moving just slightly.

My eyes jerked to her face and her eyes met mine. She was

still alive and terrified. I was by her side kneeling and grasped her hand in mine. "You're not alone." I couldn't lie and tell her it would be ok. She was dying, but I could try to offer comfort. "I'm here and I'm not going anywhere." I reached out and smoothed her hair away from her face ignoring the blood. I could hear Uncle Ray giving orders to Akira to search the area for the attacker.

There was a weak squeeze from the woman's hand as I watched her eyes start to glaze over and her chest stopped moving. Tears fell from my eyes onto her cheeks, mixing with the smeared blood.

"She's gone." I managed to choke out as I closed her eyes. That had been a savage and painful death. There were two hands on my shoulders helping me stand up gently. Uncle Ray pulled me into his arms and I let myself cry for the woman. She had only been a few hundred feet from the bar, could we have helped her somehow?

"Now, now. You held her hand and she wasn't alone, just like you told her," Uncle Ray soothed while rubbing my back, "You did what you could. We need to get back to the bar. You don't need to see this. MEPA has been called, they'll be here soon to clean this up and mask the scene from human eyes. Let's get you a drink."

$\mathcal{I}$ sat on a bar stool instead of being behind the bar for once. One of my Uncle's wolves, Chase, who had elected himself as my babysitter, poured me a finger of straight vodka and I threw it back just like I had the last two. I couldn't get warm after watching the woman pass away. Even the alcohol wasn't giving me a nice burn. We were waiting for my uncle and MEPA, Magical Entity Protection Agency, to finish up before we could leave.

"This your first dead body?" Chase asked softly as he decided to make me something without alcohol in it. I think he was trying to make a slushy with the fruits for the garnishes.

"No. I mean, yes, kind of. I've seen dead bodies, I am my mother's daughter, but I've never seen someone die so brutally before. Did they find the thing that did it?"

Chase's short, spiky, lemon yellow hair swayed left and right as he shook his head grimly. "Akira and the others who went hunting lost the scent at the 202. We figure after a few blocks whoever killed her got into a car and got on the highway." Chase was a beta, not a dominant wolf. He was usually selected to stay behind and deal with things when the pack had to hunt someone or something down. Plus, his boyfriends tended to be overly protective.

"Here," he passed me a glass that confirmed my suspicions. He had made a slushie with the leftover maraschino cherries, lemon, lime, and orange slices and simple syrup from the party. "You need sugar. That always makes the world a little brighter and I don't want you going into shock." His adorable chipmunk like cheeks smiled so cutely you would have to be a heartless asshat to say no. He usually used that smile on me when he was out of money for food or drinks.

I'm not a heartless asshat so I took the slushy, taking sips and tried to hide my grimaces at its tartness. It certainly woke me up from my funk at least. And just in time as a figure in a cloak walked into the bar. I turned around to tell the person we were closed when they pushed back their hood. I heard Chase let out a long sigh of admiration and I followed suit.

A man who could have been sculpted by the renaissance artists of old stood in front of us. His chestnut hair was shaved on the left side of his head while the rest was braided over his right shoulder. He was almost as large as Akira, muscular in all the right places and nearly as tall. His eyes were a solemn brown and, even from where I sat, I could see there was gold around his irises.

"I'm Detective Lucien from MEPA. My team's almost done with the scene, but I was told one of you was also a witness and I needed to get a statement."

That shook me out of my trance of wishing that he would remove the cloak and turn around for me so I could

see if his backside was as nice as the front. The reminder that a woman had died really took the fun out of ogling any kind of eye candy.

"That would be me, I guess." I lifted a hand up as I took a large gulp from the tart slushy for some liquid sugar courage and stood.

"Is there someplace we can talk?" The man asked politely as he walked toward the bar.

"We could use my uncle's office. I don't think he would mind." I pushed the glass back over to Chase. "Please put that in the sink, I can clean it after this. Thank you for making it for me." I smiled at Chase.

He looked between the man and me before nodding. "No problem, sweetie. I'll stay here until Ray comes back. Yell if you need me." He eyed the man, this time with suspicion instead of admiration.

I led the man through the back toward some stairs that led to a small upstairs office on the second floor. The third floor was off limits to everyone but pack members. It served as a meeting place and safe area for wolves that lost control. There was a desk in the corner with a computer for when Uncle Ray had to do inventory and taxes and a small table with a few chairs on the other side of the room. We sat at the table, the man sat with his back to the wall so he could watch the door.

"I'm Vickie, Detective." I held out my hand to him after we had settled our chairs. He looked at my hand for a moment before taking it. There was a small jolt of static electricity when our hands met. "I was outside when we heard the scream."

He pulled his hand back and from within his cloak he pulled out a pen that looked like one of those old fashioned quills and a scroll of paper. His hand left the pen and it stood on its own, ready to record our conversation. That was a handy spell. I knew Lola would love it for her job. I wondered if the detective wouldn't mind sharing the spell with me after this was over.

"Please describe to me what happened as you remember it. What were you doing outside at the time of the attack?"

I gulped and felt myself go pale. I couldn't tell him I was basically dry humping my hot werewolf best friend.

"Um," I glanced at the pen as it started to write what was said, "Do I need to tell you what I was doing before the scream?"

The man's eyes sharpened as he leaned forward. "Why? Do you have something to hide?"

"No!" My back straightened as my face flushed. "It's nothing like that. I was with Akira when we heard the scream." I continued to explain what had happened up to the point where I had gone back to the bar. I just glossed over the part where my tongue was down Akira's throat. The detective had been quiet throughout the story.

His eyes met mine as he leaned back in the chair. "Ms. Victoria," he spoke politely but firmly, "was the women able to talk at all?"

"No, her throat was ripped out. How could she have talked?" Maybe I was getting tired because I had just snapped at a MEPA detective. "I'm sorry." I sighed. "No, she didn't talk. She was terrified before she died and I couldn't do anything to help her."

"Your uncle tells me that you are the daughter of Cassandra Dwight. The one who can speak with ghosts."

I winced at my mother's name. She was such a powerhouse in the supernatural community while I was the joke of it. Why did he care about that?

"I am her daughter and yes, I can speak with ghosts." I dared him with my look to say something degrading. "I have no other powers." The pen made a swirling motion and went to the next page. I had to admit, it was a little fascinating to watch.

"I have sent out for a witch to do a summoning circle to speak with this woman's shade," witches can summon a person's shade, the person's memories, to inhabit their bodies for a small amount of time, "but if you can speak with her before the witch arrives, that would be helpful." He folded his hands together and that's when I noticed that three of his fingers on his left hand were enchanted prosthetics.

"You're a wizard." Only a magical caster of a wizard's level could do that high level of alchemy and magic to use and move enchanted prosthetics like real limbs.

He raised an eyebrow and the corner of his mouth quirked. "Yes. I am. Most of us in the MEPA crimes division are."

I blushed again and looked down. I knew that, I had just forgotten until he mentioned it.

"Can you help me?" His face went back to his professional mask of a polite powerhouse.

"I've never tried to summon one before," I answered slowly, "they've always come to me. I'm not sure if I can help you."

"That's not a no." He stood and offered his hand to me. "Let's try and see what we can come up with, hmm?"

I took his hand as I stood and that static electricity was visible as our hands met again. I flinched slightly and the detective stared down at our hands for a few moments before striding toward the door, pulling me behind, ignoring the electric sting. We went through the bar quickly, passing Chase who looked concerned, and outside to the crime scene.

The MEPA unit was parked in front of where the woman's body had been. A couple of witches were muttering spells over the ground, waving what looked like a form of smudge sticks.

"What are they doing? How are you keeping the humans away?" Curiosity got the better of me as I glanced around. The area was empty besides some wolves and the MEPA agents. I didn't even see any cars or caution tape you'd expect at a crime scene.

Detective Lucien removed his cloak, draping it over his arm and he squatted by the area where the woman had lain. I couldn't help but notice how he had a perfect bubble butt. "Look away and mirage spells. They think there is construction happening." He pointed to the area the witches were just moving from. "They are cleansing the area of bad auras and evil spirits."

I shook my head and concentrated on the subject at hand and not his bubble butt. "There aren't any ghosts, or spirits, around right now."

He looked up, meeting my eyes and I couldn't seem to look away, his eyes were gorgeous and it felt like I was falling as we continued eye contact. "Are you able to try to call her?"

I hadn't lied earlier when I had told him that ghosts came to me. I had never tried to summon them before. I wasn't quite sure how to proceed and the detective noticed my furrowed brow. He stood and walked with me a few feet away.

"I assume no one has ever worked with you before?"

"Why would they? I'm a useless dud." My tone was bitter. I usually didn't let it get to me but it was sometimes a sore spot.

The detective made a disgusted noise in the back of his throat, but it wasn't at me. It was toward the situation.

"Do you know how useful your talent would be within the MEPA?" He blew out a frustrated breath. "Have you ever meditated?"

Tilting my head, I narrowed my eyes slightly at him. "Not really, no. Why?" How could seeing ghosts help?

The mouthwatering detective took both of my hands in his. His metal fingers were cool, and he cleared his throat gruffly. "Take three deep breaths. Clear your mind of everything but the woman. Focus your mind on her and see if you can call her ghost to you."

CHAPTER 3

*H*e made it sound so easy. Meditate, clear my mind, and wham. A ghost will appear. Except, that's not what happened. All that happened was that I sat on the ground with my eyes closed and mouth cringed up in concentration. I wanted to help; I did. No one deserved what had happened to that woman and if talking to her would help, I wanted to be the one who could provide that. I thought I had felt a cold tingling in my fingertips, but when I checked around, there were no ghosts.

After another ten minutes, I opened my eyes and looked up into the detective's eyes from where I sat cross legged on the ground.

"I'm sorry. I've never called for a ghost before. They usually just appear whenever they want to." Just another reason I was the dud of the family; the disappointment of the community.

Detective Lucien helped me stand up, ignoring my groan when I tried to get the blood flowing to my legs again. I leaned against him for a moment to get my bearings. His large hands helped steady me.

"You tried, that's all I asked of you." Once he was sure I wouldn't fall, he stepped away slightly. "If you can think of anything you may have seen, even if it doesn't seem important," he handed me a card with just a number on it, "give me a call. Any time, day or night."

I nodded and placed his card in my back pocket.

"I will. Thank you." I glanced back at the area the woman's body had been. The witches were finishing their cleansing and the area looked like it was back to normal.

"Vic," Akira's voice was behind me, "are you alright?" His voice was soft and concerned. I stepped back, further away from the detective and bumped into Akira's chest as he wrapped his arms around my waist. "You're freezing." He rubbed my arms as I just realized that I was, in fact, freezing. It was already a hundred degrees outside; I had no idea why I was so cold.

"That's not weird." I made it a joke rather than thinking too hard on it. Maybe I was finally going into shock like Chase had mentioned. "Can we go home now?" I directed that at Detective Lucien.

He nodded, his eyes had narrowed slightly as they roamed over Akira and me. "Yes, please give me a call if you can think of anything. I may be in contact as well." With that he turned and walked back to the rest of the MEPA group.

Akira turned me so that I was facing him and tilted my chin up. His eyes were filled with concern, and behind that, rage over what happened to the woman basically in our backyard. I could tell his wolf was close to the surface.

"Let's go to my place." It was that simple. We could pick up where we left off, but I didn't know how I was going to explain to him, that after what just happened, I just wanted to go to sleep after a good cry. "It's quieter and you won't have to worry about Chase hovering over you like a mother hen." His lips quirked a little. "I already let him know you would be coming home with me so he wouldn't worry and try to invite himself over."

He had a point. If I went home now, Chase would be there, even if I told him no, and would want to hover and make sure I was okay, which I adored him for. But right now, I just wanted quiet.

"Akira," I took a shaky breath, "I want to discuss what happened between us; I do. But, can it wait? I really just want to cry and get some sleep."

I was suddenly airborne and cradled in his arms. Akira moved down the street to the small parking lot behind the bar.

"Hey," his voice was soothing, "I don't blame you for wanting to do that. How about some steamed milk with melon and we can sleep together? No hanky panky until you decide you want to take advantage of me." He winked after offering to make me my favorite nonalcoholic beverage. "To be honest, after this, I just want to hold you."

That last part brought blood to my cheeks again as I nodded in agreement. He set me inside of his truck and walked around to the other side. The only kind of vehicle he would drive, of course. He's Texan and a werewolf; what do you expect?

We were silent on the drive to his house. It was about a twenty minute drive from the bar. He preferred to be away from people so he had purchased a small plot of land on the outskirts of Mesa, near Apache Junction, and had set up a large manufactured house. It was just as nice, if not nicer, than a normal brick and mortar home. I knew the place like the back of my hand, having spent a lot of my free time over here with him through the years.

It was close to eight a.m., according to his dashboard clock, as we pulled up in front of his house. I couldn't hide the yawn that took over and laughed as Akira's jaw cracked open shortly after mine.

"Can we skip the drink?" We walked inside the house, quickly shutting and locking the door behind us. "I think I'm about to pass out."

"Sounds good to me." Akira could go for days without rest, any shifters could, but this situation had been draining for everyone. "You can borrow a shirt to sleep in."

"Thanks." As we walked down the hall toward the bedroom, I wondered if I should go into the guest room like I normally would. As I stopped in front of it, Akira pulled my hand toward his bedroom, the decision made for me.

His room was large. I could fit my apartment inside of it, with his en suite bathroom in the corner. His dressers were lined along the wall and in the middle of the room stood his bed. It was large and softer than a cloud. We had spent many nights watching movies, eating popcorn, and playing video games in this bed. Akira moved over to one of the smaller dressers, pulled out a large t-shirt and handed it to me.

"You can put your clothes in the hamper and I'll start the washing machine while you change." He turned, already removing his own shirt and I stopped to watch. His back muscles were a work of art. I wanted to sink my teeth into every inch of them. His hands moved to his pants and he glanced back at me, smirking. "Never knew you were a perv."

I stuttered in outrage as he laughed. I rushed over to the bathroom and slammed the door shut, leaning against it. A smile curved along my lips. I should have confessed to him sooner if this was how he was reacting to it. The smile faded. I hoped, at least, that he felt the same. I didn't want to be just another bed warmer.

It only took a few seconds to get out of my dirty clothes and into the t-shirt he had loaned me. It almost reached to my knees. I felt like a kid in it. I didn't want to wear dirty underwear so those went into the hamper as well and I would see if I could borrow a pair of boxers for the night.

Akira was putting new sheets on the bed when I walked out. He was wearing shorts and nothing else and that caused my brain to short circuit. How was that fair? He didn't seem to notice that I was struck dumb as he finished with the sheets and put the pillows and blanket back on the bed.

"Here," he walked over, "I'll start the laundry. Go ahead and get in bed."

As he left the room with the hamper of clothes, I went to his dressers, searching for his underwear drawer. I knew they'd be big but I could probably use my hair scrunchie to hold them up if I tied them to the side. I heard the washer turn, filling with water as he was putting the clothes in. I found the drawer I was looking for and hurriedly grabbed a pair of silk boxer shorts and pulled them on. Akira liked silk, he said if he didn't use silk, he would go commando.

Yep, I needed to use my scrunchie. I pulled my ponytail out and tied the scrunchie around a fistful of fabric on one side of the shorts. That would have to do. I was sliding under the blanket when Akira came back into the room and I blinked at the look on his face. It was almost embarrassed?

"Erm," he cleared his throat, "I didn't think about it, but, uh, do you need a pair of my shorts?" He must have seen my underwear and instead of blushing, I couldn't stop the laugh that bubbled up. He looked so flustered and embarrassed.

"I borrowed a pair of your boxers, if that's ok."

His eyes filled with heat again and he stalked toward the bed. A foot away he stopped and visibly shuddered.

"Damn, Vic. I know we're both tired but that's hot. I like you wearing my clothes."

That had to be a male thing because I had read similar lines in my romance books. Males and their clothes.

"Get in the bed, dork." I looked away. I was tired and if we started something, I was pretty sure I'd fall asleep during it. "Can we cuddle?"

He was on top of me before I finished my question, his lips bruising mine as I gasped in surprise. His tongue slid in and my hands dug into his back, making tiny nail prints and a moan ripped from my throat. And just like that, he rolled off me, pulling me while his arms surrounded me. I could feel how hard he was but he made no more moves.

"I'm right here. You can sleep. We'll talk more in the morning. It's been a long night."

With that reminder, the lust he had dragged out of me vanished with images of the woman on the ground. I laid my head on his arm and looked up at him.

"Akira," I touched his lips with my fingers. "Thank you for understanding."

His tongue licked at my fingertips teasingly. "No problem, doll. Get some sleep."

I wanted to stay awake but I had already started to doze off the second he had wrapped his arms around me. I finally felt safe for the first time since we heard that scream. I wanted to tell him that, but my eyelids were heavy as I drifted off.

The smell of burnt coffee and eggs tickled my nose as I woke up with my face buried in silk covered pillows. My brows furrowed as I tried to remember how I ended up in this soft cocoon of heaven. That's when it came rushing back. The dead woman and staying at Akira's place.

Akira. I sat up quickly, looking around his room, I touched my lips remembering how we had kissed, our flirting finally evolving.

"Hey, Vic," Akira's gravelly voice echoed from the front of the house, "breakfast is almost done."

"R-right. I'll be there in a moment." Damn that werewolf hearing. He'd known the second I woke up. I went to the bathroom and while I washed my hands, I looked into the mirror.

At first, I thought I had to be hallucinating; there was no way the shower stall was covered in blood. I blinked, but it was still there. I turned around and it was still covered in what looked like blood. I took the few steps needed to reach it and touched a tile, trailing my finger down, but no mark appeared and my finger came away clean. Well, that was weird. Maybe I was still a little messed up from the crime scene.

"Vic?" There was a knock on the door. "You alright?"

"Yeah, sorry." I glanced to the door and back and the blood, or whatever it is, had vanished. "Coming." I opened the door and looked up at Akira's face and smiled. "Morning, handsome. You burned the coffee again, didn't you?"

A slight flush graced his cheeks as Akira looked away. "Only once. The new batch is fine."

I laughed and took his arm. "Thank you for making breakfast."

His eyes had softened as he searched mine. For what, I'm not sure, but whatever he saw seemed to reassure him. He pulled me with him and we went into the kitchen to sit at the small breakfast nook that looked out into the backyard. The table had two plates filled with werewolf breakfast essentials and a bowl of fruit next to the plate that must have been designated for me.

"You got fruit for me?" He didn't normally have it in his house. He tended to hate fruit. He called it girly food and he wouldn't eat it unless he was forced to. Butterflies warmed within my stomach and I smiled. "Thanks."

Akira sat across from me and began to eat. "I needed groceries anyways; I thought you might like it with breakfast." He must have gotten up a few hours ago to go grocery shopping and be back in time to have breakfast made by the time I woke up. It would have been busy since it was almost two in the afternoon.

I popped a piece of honeydew melon in my mouth and almost moaned out loud. "It's cold and very juicy."

A snort was my reply as we both dug into our breakfast. It wasn't long before Akira was finished before me.

"So, Vic, I'm going to start and you can just listen, alright?" He didn't wait for my reply. "I want you to know that last night, before that woman's murder, I was serious. I wanted to be the one to tell you first." He took a sip of his coffee. "I've been in love with you for years. Ever since I joined the pack, but you were barely sixteen." His eyes met mine. "There was no way I was going to pursue that. You were still a child, so I buried those feelings and was content with being your friend."

I had stopped eating the strawberry I had picked up. It fell onto the plate with a small splat. I stared at him wide eyes. He'd been in love with me as long as I had been in love with him?

"When I had been dating Lola and you had gotten so mad at us that one time, it nearly broke my heart. If she hadn't broken up with me the next day, I would have done it. And when I beat the crap out of Shax, the douchebag, I wanted to kill him for touching you." He took a breath. "If we move forward, I can't go back to the way it was before, if you happen to change your mind halfway through. Ray won't like it, but I will talk to him about it."

"So," I had to clear my throat, "You love me, too?"

Akira threw his head back in a laugh. "Yes, I love you, you dork."

"I love you. I've always loved you." I spoke quietly, but let him see I was serious. "My family will just have to deal."

Akira stood abruptly and came to kneel next to my chair; his hands cupping my face. "You've done it now."

My laughter was cut off as he kissed me. Our lips just brushing each other as we sought more. I had just started to press into the kiss more as he pulled back. A scowl of irritation lit his face as he pulled out his phone from his back pocket.

"This is starting to become a theme." He grumbled as he answered the phone. "Yes, Ray?" There was a momentary pause as whatever Uncle Ray said caused Akira's face to become serious. "I'll be there soon." He hung up and looked at me, a strained smile on his lips.

"It's alright. Pack comes first."

"For now. I'll talk to Ray about us while I'm there."

"Shouldn't you talk to my parents, instead? If you're going the whole old tradition route?" I couldn't help but tease him a little.

Akira scoffed and kissed my cheek. "Brat. I'll be back as soon as I can."

I watched him leave and finished my plate. I decided to do the dishes. It was only right since he had cooked breakfast. It didn't take long and let my mind wander. I kept thinking on the dead woman and the blood but not blood in the shower earlier. I decided to go see if it would happen again.

It was only a minute later and I stood in the bathroom with my hands on my hips. Everything looked normal and no matter how many times I blinked or scrunched my nose, the blood didn't return. It was starting to annoy me when I heard someone clear their throat behind me.

Turning around slowly my eyes met brilliant hazel green eyes. It was the woman from the alley. The ghost floated in front of the doorway, her white dress floating around her knees. She had a heart shaped face with long hair. She must have been a heartbreaker when she was alive.

"Hi." I had to swallow to try to fight the dry mouth that suddenly occurred.

"You wanted to talk to me last night. I felt your call." Her voice was deep, deeper than I would have imagined her to have.

She had felt my call? That's when I remembered when Detective Lucien had me meditate.

"You felt me call you? Really?"

She blinked at me and nodded. "It was dark where I was and cold too. I heard your voice and I followed it here."

I had to sit down. I had actually called a ghost. I had never done that before and honestly didn't think it had worked. I walked over to the tub and sat on the edge.

"What's your name?" I watched as the ghost floated in front of the mirror checking out her face and running a hand through her hair.

"Siobal." She lifted her chin, tilting her face to the side. "Being dead has done wonders for my complexion."

"That's obviously what's important."

She glanced back at me and smiled. "No snarky comments needed. I'm dead, just like I foresaw, and met you."

Say what now? "Wait, what?"

Siobal laughed and if the temperature didn't drop in the room, I was the Easter bunny. "I am, or was, a clairvoyant. A sex clairvoyant to be more precise." Her lips were turned up in an amused smile.

"Now you're just making things up."

"I'm telling the truth. You can look up my website." She was having too much fun with me but I grabbed my cellphone and looked up the website she gave me.

Her website was colorful and she did advertise herself as a clairvoyant with a twist. She would read your future but, in order to do that, she would need sex to generate her gift. I looked at her blankly.

"Really?"

"Yes, really. I had my best visions after using sex as a catalyst to power them. Not to mention, I was also a third succubus, on my mother's side. Grandma was one of the last free demons on the Earth when she passed away in the 1800's. So, it fueled my visions and fed me." She wiggled her eyebrows together and that was an impressive feat I had never been able to do.

I shook my head. "Back to the part where you died. You saw that and didn't try to stop it?"

"Of course I tried to stop it. I did everything to prevent it, but the lady fates were determined, so I died. But you showed up and were kind to me at the end. I stopped being afraid. Thank you for that."

"You shouldn't thank me. We couldn't help you."

"You weren't meant to save me but you were meant to be there so I could help you stop this killer."

CHAPTER 4

"Me? Help you stop the killer?" It took me a few seconds to formulate a response. "I'm a bartender, shouldn't you talk to the witches who are going to summon you from the MEPA?"

Siobal waved her hand in front of her face dismissively. "They don't have the power to bring me back to this plane like you do. Only person who can see me is you. So that means you get to pass along my information." She grinned, almost devilishly, and floated up to the ceiling. "Oh, I should let you know, because of how I was killed and how you summoned me," she flipped upside down like a Spiderman movie but her dress didn't move from her knees, "to keep me here, I am using your life energy. So, you'll need help from that really sexy MEPA detective to stay alive until he catches the killer with our help. I'm going to go explore, I'll be back later. Tootles!"

"Wait, one second, Siobal! What do you mean?" I stood and yelled, but the room was empty. "What the hell is going on?"

Frustrated and confused, I picked up my phone in the kitchen. I had put the detective's information in my contacts last night after he gave me his card. He seemed to know a lot more about ghosts than most people so maybe he could shine a light on what Siobal was talking about. I put the phone on speaker as I waited for him to pick up.

"This is Detective Lucien." At his low voice I had a hard time forming words for a few seconds. "Hello?"

I shook my head and answered, "Detective Lucien? This is Vickie, from last night at the bar?"

"Ah, yes. How can I help you? Is everything ok?"

"Um, well, not really."

There was a brief silence. "Vickie?" His voice had softened. "Are you alright?"

It didn't take long before I had explained what had occurred to the detective. "Why does she think that she is draining, what did she call it? My life energy?"

"It's concerning. She was a powerful clairvoyant, thanks in part, to her power drawing on her incubus heritage. It's possible that has something to do with what she's talking about. Let me reach out and get some answers. Can you meet me in two hours?"

We agreed to meet at his office in Tempe in two hours. He told me to not worry, but how could I not? My whole world turned upside-downside within the past twenty four hours. Some of it was good, oh so good. My thoughts momentarily drifted to Akira, but a lot of it was scary. Siobal being murdered for one and her ghost saying I had summoned terrified me.

I sat on Akira's bed cross-legged and went through my phone. I pulled up a photo of my family. Mom and Dad stood a foot apart. My little brother, Jacob was in the center smiling like nothing bothered him. My older brother, Samuel, towered next to my dad. And me, next to Samuel. Everyone in my family had strong magic. Mom being a witch, Dad a fox shifter; Jacob being the golden boy, was a fox shifter and witch hybrid, while Samuel was a werewolf from Dad's first marriage, and then there is me. The ghost dud, so lovingly nick named by Jacob, with no magic beyond seeing ghosts.

As I was off in my own world again, a call came through from Akira. I answered it quickly.

"Hey, Vic, it seems something has happened that's making Ray twitchy. He's called for the whole pack and it looks like I'll be here for a while yet."

"Oh, well, that's ok. I have today off and I can call for a rideshare to pick up my car." I needed to get home to change and meet up with the detective. "I'm meeting up with that detective from last night in a few hours."

"Why? Are you ok?" Akira's voice sharpened.

"I'm alright. I just have a follow up with him. I promise to tell you about it tonight."

Akira was silent as he thought for a few moments. "I don't like you going out alone with this killer still loose, but as long as you're home before night fall, it should be alright. Why don't I come over tonight?"

I giggled softly. "Are you worried or do you want in my pants, Mr. Wolf?"

"Oh," his voice turned into that low growl that sent happy shivers along my spine, "I most definitely want in your pants." And just like that, I was close to panting, the asshat.

"I'll see you after we get done for the day." If my voice was a bit deeper it was his fault, not mine. "Be safe." I hung up and pulled up my rideshare app, ordering a ride as soon as possible.

It didn't take long to get my clothes from the dryer and get dressed. I had just pulled on my shirt when the app sent an alert letting me know my ride was outside. I locked up Akira's house, using the key he had given me a few years ago, and got into the back of the car.

The driver was a kind faced older woman who introduced herself as Janice. Janice was polite and was the first rideshare driver I had who actually paid attention to the motor laws, which meant it took a bit longer to get to my studio apartment a few blocks away from the bar. I couldn't get annoyed though because she kept up a good conversation. She even offered to wait for me and would take me to the bar so I could get my own car. I took her up on that offer because, even though it was only a few blocks away, it was already 102 degrees out and the humidity was rising. You can call me lazy if you like, but I loved my AC. I was quick to change and grab my phone charger and backpack that I carry instead of a purse. I ran back outside to Janice. She dropped me off in front of my car with a friendly wave and offered to pick me up again whenever I needed.

Once I was in my car, I was able to turn on the AC full blast and I headed out to the address Detective Lucien had given me in Tempe. I got there in record time, ignoring speed limits like every Arizonian I knew, minus Janice. The address led me to a non-descript group of two story buildings near the I-10 and Baseline. They encircled a beautiful, yet small, courtyard that had multiple water fountains around the area and a small pond in the middle. Detective Lucien's office was straight through the courtyard and as I walked through the door, a receptionist greeted me.

"Hello, I have an appointment, I think, with Detective Lucien."

His eyes focused on me and I noticed when he blinked, it was a vertical blink. He must have been a kappa. "Victoria? He's expecting you, down the hall and to the left."

I thank him with a nod as I walked to the door the receptionist mentioned and saw Detective Lucien's name on the side of it. I knocked quietly a few times.

"Come in." His voice was distracted.

When I opened the door, I had to blink a few times. The office looked like a tornado had blown in and decided to make itself at home. The detective sat at a desk near the only window and it was covered in random papers. His face was furrowed in concentration, looking at a folder of paperwork and his hair was disheveled, like he hadn't slept. It was kind of cute actually.

"Hello, Detective Lucien. I'm not late, am I?"

He glanced up and his eyes widened slightly. I could have sworn his cheeks flushed. "Ah, Victoria. Has it been two hours already? My apologies. Please, come sit." He waved at a chair filled with paperwork, but as he gestured, the paperwork flew off to a corner of the room.

"Nice office." I grinned, dodging piles of paperwork and sat in the chair, facing him. "It's not what I expected from a MEPA cop."

A smile quirked at his lips as he ran a hand through his hair. "Yeah, sorry about the mess. The papers are tagged so I can summon them but I'm not good with physical organization."

"Obviously." I couldn't stop myself from laughing.

A real smile spread across his face and it transformed him from handsome to breathtaking. "I have been doing a little research on Siobal and a coworker pulled some records about cases where we worked with shades to see if we could find anything about what she told you had any merit to it." He sighed and leaned back into his chair. "I hate to say that I haven't found anything concrete. No one has ever interacted with ghosts as you do. As far as what Siobal mentioned of draining your life energy, do you feel any different?"

I shook my head and shrugged. "Not really. Just confused."

"Well, that's because I haven't been in this plane except for now and when we first talked." Siobal was suddenly next to Detective Lucien, looking into his face. "Oh, he is gorgeous. First the wolf and now this wizard. You should hit both." She looked over at me and grinned. "I bet they're both great kissers."

I flushed and glared at her. "Were you always such a pervert?"

The detective looked at me confused, "What?"

Siobal laughed and sat on the desk as I groaned. "Sorry Detective Lucien. Um, Siobal is here."

"Just call me Lucien, please." He glanced around his office. "I don't sense any change in the air."

"Trust me," I said dryly, "she's here. She seems to like you."

"Fascinating." Lucien sat forward, lacing his fingers together. "Well, let's ask her about what she means about your life energy."

I looked at her and raised my eyebrow. She stuck her tongue out at me.

"Like I said before, you summoned me and to keep me here, I am draining you until I am no longer needed. Which means we need to catch the person who killed me, and quick."

"And what about making sure I don't die?"

"Oh, that. Well, I would say sex but you're not incubi so that wouldn't work most likely. I suggest working with Mr. Sexy here to figure that out. I'll do my best not to be here more than you need me, though. When I'm not in this plane, I'm not using your energy."

"So basically, to be here she has to use my energy. She doesn't know how to stop me from dying. She said to work with you on that. She's here to help catch the killer."

The detective was writing down what I said. "I'm not sure how, but I will help you. This is partially my fault; I encouraged you to try to summon her. I can't let you become harmed for trying to help me." He paused. "But, Siobal's help could be invaluable. Will you help me? And don't feel pressured to say yes, I will help you regardless."

"Oh, you have to help them, or I won't be able to move on." Siobal's stare was hard.

"Of course, I will help you, Lucien. And you too, Siobal. I want this killer to pay for what he did." Not to mention getting time to hang out with detective hottie was a plus.

He nodded and stood. "That's great news. Why don't we start with an interview with Siobal? After, we can head to the first murder scene." Lucien pulled out his spelled quill and paper. "Please repeat to me exactly what she says. Siobal, please tell me what you remember."

"It started three weeks ago," I started to repeat her words shortly after she started, "I had a vision of my death after seeing a news report from MEPA about the first death that happened in Central Phoenix."

"We didn't find the first body until three weeks ago and the body count is climbing. Six total, including Siobal's."

"Six? In only three weeks? That's a body almost every three or four days."

Lucien nodded, "That's right. Sorry to interrupt, please continue."

Siobal continued to explain how she had taken steps to try to avoid her death. Even going as far as getting on a plane to Colorado two days before the night of her death.

"When she woke up after falling asleep in a hotel in Colorado, she found she was back in her own bed in Scottsdale and she knew she couldn't run from her fate. That fate was to be killed and help me and the MEPA capture this killer. If we don't, he'll keep killing until he exposes the supernatural world to the human world, dooming us all."

My tongue felt heavy as I finished the interview, Siobal looked drained as well. She looked me in the eye with her next statement.

"The killer is supernatural, but not one that any of us have encountered in many centuries." With that she nodded and disappeared.

When I told Lucien what she had just said, he frowned. "A supernatural we have not seen in centuries? That could be any number of ancients that went into hiding when the human's technology started to overwhelm the more magic sensitive."

"She's left for now; I think she got tired."

Lucien stood and grabbed some keys that were in a small drawer in his desk. "Well, Victoria, care to ride with me? I'd like to take you to the first scene. If any of the victim's ghosts are still there, they might be able to provide valuable information. I know it's late so we can pick up where we leave off tomorrow. My team is still going over Siobal's townhouse, so it's best we wait to go there until they've given the okay."

I took a deep breath but agreed. I was used to seeing and talking to ghosts, but the idea of seeing a ghost where they were killed sent a shiver of fear down my spine. I wanted to help Siobal and Lucien so I was going to suck it up and do it. Plus, if my help lead to catching this killer, I wasn't going to say no.

"What do you say to some food on the way?" Lucien held his

office door open for me and led the way through the beautiful court-yard. "It's near dinner so we shouldn't run into any traffic, at least."

"What, no donuts?" I grinned at him as he walked us to a blue sedan and opened up the passenger door for me.

"That's for tomorrow morning." He winked as he shut the door and went to the driver's side of the car. I was laughing as he got in. "I actually love donuts except I don't have them except once a week. Otherwise, I'll eat them all day, every day and that could end up badly for me when I have to chase a bad guy down the street."

"You're not what I expected from a MEPA detective." He was serious with a sense of humor.

"Let me guess. You thought we were all old men with long white beards and flowing robes?" His grin had a flash of teeth in it and I felt that tug in my inner core again.

"Something like that."

"Not long ago, you would have been right." He pulled onto the highway and started toward Central Phoenix. "A decade ago, multiple wizards who had been with MEPA since it was created, retired. That opened up positions for the younger generation to take over. My father was one of those old men with the white beards. He is a hit as Dumbledore now at Halloween parties."

I laughed again and looked out the window. "I've never met anyone besides you from MEPA. I'm usually either at my uncle's bar or with friends playing video games."

He looked at me quickly before focusing on driving. "I had a question about that. I pulled your records." He passed several cars as he got into the HOV lane. "You were in the top five percent of your class in high school. You were in multiple clubs and had offers for scholarships that would be the envy of any child. Why are you a bartender?"

I picked at a piece of nonexistent lint on my pants. He went for the serious questions right off the bat. "You know who my parents and brothers are. Anything I do would be outshined by any of their accomplishments. Not to mention, anything I do, is never enough for my mother. I had planned to go to NAU, live in the dormitories and attempt to live without the supernatural community as I tried to figure out what I wanted to do with my life, but," my voice had a nasty bite to it, "that would blemish the family reputation. Jacob needed to be the one to go to college and have the light on him." I smiled at Lucien. "So, Uncle offered to let me be a bartender and I never looked back. It let me move out into my studio, away from my parents and closer to my uncle and best friends. I actually like what I do. The hours kind of suck sometimes, but for the most part, it works. I haven't found anything else that piques my interest, so for now, I'll stick to being a bartender."

"I envy your carefree attitude. My father had decided my life before I was even born. You know that most of us wizards aren't born the natural way."

I tilted my head. I hadn't known that.

"Most wizards are born when our fathers cast a spell on our mothers' stomach that penetrates the womb, no sex needed. After we're born, most of our mothers' minds are wiped and our fathers raise us. I'm one of the lucky ones," his voice was tender when he spoke, "my mother is still in my life."

"So," I cleared my throat, "that's kind of creepy. I'm not going to lie. Wizards don't have sex?"

That caused Lucien to laugh so hard that he had to take a sip of water from a bottle from the backseat. "No, we have sex. I have sex." He winked at me and I got warm. "It's just some of the older generation tend to believe we come out stronger if we are spelled into our mothers' wombs versus the natural way of conception."

I knew I was blushing, so I looked out the window again to hide it. We had been driving for almost fifteen minutes and were turning off the highway onto the 7th Ave exit.

"The first murder," Lucien changed the subject thankfully, "was a male satyr who was working the night shift as a security guard for some apartments. Unlike Siobal, the other victims weren't found right away so the killer," he paused as if he was trying to find a way to describe the next thing, "the killer raped the victims after they were killed. After that he took different parts of their bodies; mostly their eyes and tongues. Two of the victims are also missing their hearts."

Well, that was gross and gruesome. "Like, the killer ate them?"

"Or took them as souvenirs." Lucien pulled into a Wendy's drive thru, "and with that in mind, what would you like to eat?"

I looked at him, my mouth gaping like a confused fish. He had just talked about disembowelment and eating people and now wanted to order food. He must have seen my look because he chuckled and ordered two small vanilla Frosties, a large fry, a large coke, and lemon lime soda.

"How did you know I would eat a vanilla Frosty with fries?"

"Because, my dear Victoria," he paid cash and asked for the receipt, "if you didn't, you'd be the real monster here." He handed me the drink carrier with the drinks and Frosties and the small bag with the fries. "Was I wrong? Are you a monster?" He raised his eyebrow at me as he pulled out of the drive thru and back onto the street.

I laughed getting the Frosties together and handed him a dipped fry. "No, you weren't wrong. I love vanilla Frosties with French fries."

Our fingers touched and that feeling of electricity from before jolted through me. He popped the fry into his mouth humming happily.

"So, besides hoping the ghosts can ID the killer, is there anything else you're looking for? Shouldn't their shades have answers?"

"Yes, I am looking to see if they remember anything out of the ordinary, any strangers hanging around them. Anything that could give a clue as to who our killer is. Shades can only answer yes or no questions. If we don't ask the right question, we won't have an answer."

We ate our fries and Frosties in silence after that and we soon pulled into an underground parking garage that belonged to a building full of high rise apartments. I think I would have to work three years before I could afford a down payment for a place here. It was fancy with a capital F. Lucien parked on the second level near the stairs.

"The scene has been spelled clean, but I can pull it up with a mirage spell if you need to look at it." He led us to a parking spot that was blocked off with construction equipment next to the stairs. "Let's see if the victims' ghost is anywhere. When we summoned his shade, he didn't answer any questions."

"Lucien," I looked around warily and had to be honest with him, "I don't know if this will work. It took hours for Siobal to show up."

"That's alright. I don't want you to try to summon him. I would just like to see if he's here. I don't want you summoning anymore ghosts until we figure out what Siobal meant about your life energy. Your life is non-negotiable."

I laughed at him. "I bet you say that to all the girls."

"Mm. Only the important ones." He was casting the mirage spell facing the other way, so he missed when I tripped after he said that. This man was good at flattery and I don't think he even noticed. The mirage spell activated and all thoughts emptied as I looked at the scene before me.

The victim was young, maybe just over twenty, and wore the apartment security guard outfit. In death his glamour had disappeared and you could see his furred legs and hooves. Like Lucien had said, his eyes were missing and his mouth was opened forever in a scream.

"He was so young." I whispered softly. "How is that fair?" I felt a cool breeze lift my hair from behind and my head felt strange for a moment.

"Yeah, dying really sucked." A voice sporting an Irish accent spoke next to me. The victim's ghost had come out as soon as the spell was finished. He stood at my height and waved at me. "I'm Tyler and I guess I'm dead."

I nodded at him. "I'm sorry, Tyler. You were killed and I know this might be weird, but I was hoping you could tell me if you remember what happened or if you remember anything being weird?"

He looked confused before answering slowly. "I don't remember. I think I was late to my shift. I was always doing that. I think I saw a bright flash of red light and that was followed by so much pain." His voice had moved to a whisper. "So much pain. I prayed it would end because it seemed to go on forever. It finally did, I guess."

I reached out to touch his cheek and was surprised when I was able to. He felt solid. I must have shocked him because he just stared at me. "You're no longer in pain, that's what matters. Detective Lucien, the guy over there, is going to find the person who did this to you." I waved over to where he stood watching me silently.

Tyler looked like he was about to cry, but he didn't and just nodded. "I'm sorry, I don't remember anything except that bright red light. Everything else seemed normal. I had just had a fun night out with my friends the night before at a few bars in Gilbert."

"Wait, Gilbert? Did you go to Supe's Karaoke Bar?" I don't remember seeing Tyler, perhaps he went there on my night off. There was only one supernatural friendly bar in Gilbert.

He nodded. "Yeah, that was one of them. It was fun. I thought it would be great to go back some time. It had been my first time there with my friends." He glanced down at the spelled image of his body and up at me after a moment. "We got into a bit of a scuffle with some regulars and I got hit with a spell." He pointed to his right hand in the image. It was curled as if he were fighting something but I could see a black mark in his palm that traveled up his arm, it almost looked like a birthmark.

"Lucien," I pointed out to him what Tyler said. "He also went to my uncles bar before coming to work late."

Lucien knelt in front of the body image and took a picture with his phone. "We assumed that this was a birthmark." He stood and faced me. "Two victims near your uncle's bar could be a coincidence. I doubt it."

Tyler moved away but turned back to look at me after a few

moments. "I'm really tired. Could you tell my mom that I'm sorry and I love her?"

I could only nod as I fought not to cry. "Promise."

"I hope you catch him." With that, Tyler disappeared.

"Tyler's ghost left. He wants us to tell his mom that he's sorry and he loves her." I wiped away the tears that fell even as I tried to hold them back. "How do you do this?" I looked up at Lucien as he walked over to stand next to me. He reached up and used a thumb to wipe more tears away.

"I do this so that more Tyler's don't show up." He waited a moment and when I just cried, he pulled me into his arms and held me close. His right hand held the back of my head to his chest. "Go ahead. Let it out." His voice was soft and soothing.

I'm not sure how long we stood there while I cried for Tyler, his mom, and also, Siobal. They had their lives taken from them violently and had done nothing to deserve it. The whole time I cried Lucien held me close and rubbed my back.

After a few minutes a car drove behind us, honking their horn causing me to jump away. "Oh! I'm sorry. Your poor shirt!" I had caused a large wet spot on Lucien's shirt. I felt my face go red and if steam were visible, he'd probably see it pouring from my ears.

"It's quite alright. I offered, remember?" Lucien chuckled and offered his arm. "I don't even have to dispel the mirage; our honker did that for us." The spell must have disappeared the second a human was near.

I put my hand in the crook of his arm and was silent as I started to think about multiple things all at once. How Tyler and Siobal had both been at or near the bar, how Siobal had said that the killer would continue and get worse until we catch him, and, if I were being honest with myself, how attracted I was to the detective. That last thought made me feel guilty.

I was in love with Akira and he said he was in love with me too. We were going to finally have sex tonight, if everything went according to plan, and yet, here I was, wanting Lucien to hold me again. I sighed rubbing my temples. My life had never been so hectic before and I wasn't sure I was going to be able to keep up.

"Penny for your thoughts?" Lucien's hand appeared in my vision, holding a penny between his metal fingers and that made me laugh. I looked up at him and noticed we had gotten into the car and were already on the move.

"Thanks, but they aren't even worth that much." I took the penny and turned it over in my palm. "We're headed to the second victim's scene now?" I glanced at the clock and saw that the time had flown by. It was nearly nine.

"No, I think this will be the only place we go to today and can pick up tomorrow, if you have time. I have new information about Tyler, thanks to you, that I can work on tonight."

"I have a shift tomorrow night, but I can help you during the day, as long as I'm back at the bar before my shift starts."

Lucien nodded at me before playing chicken with a car turning the opposite way. It was like he got off on dangerous driving. "That's doable. We could start midmorning. Would you like me to drop you off at my office or take you elsewhere?"

"Let me text someone really quick." I pulled out my phone and noticed I had a few text messages from Akira and Lola.

I responded to Lola who wanted to hear about the night before when she had left early. I promised to follow up with her later. Akira's texts were slightly disappointing because he and a few of the pack had been ordered to patrol around the bar area for the night. So, no sex, at least for tonight. Back to using my handy dandy tentacle toy. At least he said he'd be free the next night.

"How about you just drop me off at home? I can catch a rideshare to your office tomorrow." I didn't like driving at night unless I had to, I didn't have the best eyesight.

"That's fine. I can pick you up tomorrow morning, if that works?" He flashed a grin at me that warmed my toes.

For the rest of the ride we made small talk. I was enjoying learning about the detective; he wasn't at all what I thought a

MEPA agent would be like. He was only a year younger than Akira and his favorite food was steak, something he and Akira had in common.

"What happened to your fingers?" I was curious and the question just kind of popped out and I winced slightly, but before I could apologize and take it back, Lucien chuckled softly.

"It was a couple of years ago," he paused as he took a left into my apartment complex, "I was still in training when we had a call about a rampaging troll. He had been spelled to sleep a few decades ago and the spell wore off. He was not a happy camper."

He pulled in front of my apartment building, parked, and he turned on the overhead light. He shifted to look at me, that electric zing almost visible. He held out his left hand and I took it in my hands tilting his metal fingers toward the light. They looked like stainless steel but they were spelled so they were probably stronger than steel. He wiggled them for me and they moved just like any other finger.

"I got too close and the troll grabbed me. Threw me around like a ragdoll before attempting to eat me."

I sat up straighter. "No. You were almost eaten? Was his breath rank? It had to be after years of not brushing. Did you get some kind of infection?"

Lucien laughed which sent those shivers through me again. The skin around his eyes crinkled slightly as he laughed. "Yeah, his breath was horrible. My dad and his partner managed to freeze him for a few seconds and I got away, but not before the troll bit down on my hand as the freeze spell wore off. Luckily, our healers are top notch. I only lost the three fingers and these prosthetics are basically the same thing. I don't even notice the drain on my magic anymore; it's such a small amount."

Only a wizard would say a constant magical drain on their resources would be an insignificant amount that they weren't bothered by it. I couldn't hold back my eye roll and Lucien's mouth turned into a smirk.

"I know. Sounds like I'm bragging. Maybe I am. Does it impress you?"

"Well, such a strong, magically muscled man such as yourself must impress all the girls in the office. My little heart is all a pitter-patter." I fluttered my eyelashes at him which caused him to snort.

He leaned forward and I froze as his lips neared mine. Was there a flash of heat in his eyes as they met mine? Was he going to kiss me? What would I do? I would kiss him back, wouldn't I? I closed my eyes anticipating the kiss, the kiss didn't come, there was just the sound of the door clicking open. My eyes jerked open and Lucien was back in his seat smiling at me. His warm chocolate eyes with the golden circle hue took my breath away. He had opened my door by leaning over me. He hadn't gotten close to kiss me. Damn it.

"I'll see you tomorrow morning." His voice was husky and he took a second to clear his throat. "I have your number. I'll call you when I'm on the way."

"Right." I tried not to show my disappointment and unbuckled my seatbelt. "I'll see you tomorrow. Try not to wake up any more trolls." Oh, I really said something that lame, didn't I?

"Will do." Amusement laced his reply as I stepped out of the sedan and closed the door.

He waved as he backed up and left the parking lot. His rearview lights disappeared around the corner and I sighed. The detective was dreamy and I couldn't wait to spend more time with him.

CHAPTER 5

I was clutching the arm rest as Lucien sped on the frontage road, it made me miss Janice's careful driving. Lucien drove like the devil. We were headed toward a Gilbert neighborhood where the second victim had been murdered in their home.

Lucien had picked me up a few minutes after eleven in the morning. I had barely woken up when I had gotten his text that he was on his way over. I managed to get my jeans on just as he knocked on the door. When I opened the door, he was there in tight jeans and a button down blue shirt.

"Manna from heaven?" I had grabbed the to-go cup he held out to me and inhaled the hot liquid. "Oh hot!" I still gulped it down as he laughed at me anyway. It was hot and it was caffeinated. It was all I cared about as I struggled to form coherent thoughts. I wasn't used to being up until at least noon on the days I worked and these past few days were catching up to me.

Lucien tilted his head slightly and his lips curled up sending a pleasant wake up shiver through me.

"You know, most folks blow on it a few times before drinking it down." Oh, he had sass. I could give that right back.

"You know, most decent folks bring a muffin with the coffee they bring." I smirked at him but paused as he held up a bag of pastries. "Oh. Well. You should have led with that." He just snickered at me as we left my apartment and got on the road.

Lucien had handed me the victims' files after I had buckled in so I could familiarize myself with the information in case any of the ghosts were there. The second victim had been an older female lynx shifter. I had never met her but I recognized her name from the karaoke award wall in the bar. Uncle Ray made sure I dusted the pictures on that wall at least once a week. She had won several karaoke contests years ago in the eighties and early nineties. I think her name was Sheila.

"Lucien," I bit my thumbnail nervously, "this is weird. The second victim used to be a frequent flyer at the bar in the eighties."

"What? Are you sure?" He glanced over at me briefly.

"Yes, her pictures are up on the awards wall. It just took me a few to remember."

"Twice is a coincidence. Three is a pattern." Lucien mused as he made a left turn. "I can't believe that his hunting ground is the bar except it's looking more like a possibility as we go along. His victims have all been random as far as we can tell and most of them had little magical power so they were easy targets. Siobal is the only one that was killed that had any remarkable magic. I think these victims were just a warm up for whatever he's really after."

"And that's not a terrifying thought at all." I licked my lips as they had gone dry. If the killer really was targeting customers at the bar, I needed to tell Uncle Ray. We might need to close the bar until the killer was caught. I flipped through the other victims' files. There was another shifter female, a male desert troll (a cousin to the type of the troll that had eaten Lucien's fingers), and a male vampire who was only a decade turned. None of the names or pictures looked familiar, I would see if I could get copies to see if Uncle Ray recognized the other victims.

We pulled into a quiet neighborhood and the house was located at the end of a cul-de-sac. It was an older ranch style house and the yard was covered in garden gnome statues. The woman obviously had a fun sense of humor when I noticed she'd put some of the gnomes together to look like an orgy. I couldn't help giggling as we exited the car when Lucien raised his eyebrow and gave me a sexy smirk. Her neighbors must have either hated her or loved her.

We went inside the house, turning on the lights. The front hall smelled of bleach, sage, and lemon. The smell continued through the house as we walked toward the back bedrooms, hints of sage wafting from the corners.

"The killer broke through the backdoor and attacked our victim as she slept. As far as we can tell, she didn't even fight back." Lucien opened the master bedroom door and muttered, "Revelare." The mirage spell started rippling as images from the scene appeared and I felt the muffin fighting its way back up.

Sheila, being a shifter, didn't appear to be older than forty five but was most likely double that. She lay spread eagle on the bed, eyes gouged out, and mouth opened in a, now silent, scream. But what was more disturbing, and causing my stomach to threaten to up-chuck, was that her chest cavity had been pried open. Her ribs splayed out like someone opened a cage. Her heart was missing.

I had to look at the wall for several moments to fight back the bile that kept coming up. Lucien stood beside me rubbing my back, making soothing sounds.

"This kill was the most violent." Lucien muttered softly as I gulped in air. "My team tells me that she was awake when he tore her heart out. The blood patterns around the body confirm that." He stepped away from me and moved closer to the body image. "He didn't take the eyes or tongue until he was done with the body. We have evidence of penetration from each murder scene but we have yet to find any traces of bodily fluid from our killer." Lucien sounded frustrated at that. "It's as if he doesn't exist."

I closed my eyes when I felt a soft breeze, my head felt a bit lighter, similar to what I felt before Tyler's ghost showed up. "He was so angry." A voice said from the corner of the room. "I woke up and this shadow was choking me with a hand while another tore my clothes off." I walked around the bed and saw the ghost, Sheila's ghost, huddled in the corner, her arms wrapped around her knees. I kneeled in front of her and touched her knee, only slightly surprised when I could touch her, like I had with Tyler.

"Sheila," I whispered, not wanting to spook her, "can you tell me what happened? Did you see his face?"

She looked up at me, tear tracks visibly running down her cheeks. "I never saw his face. He wore a black hood. He had red claws or maybe they were red from my blood." She whispered. "He tore open my chest after he bit my tongue out. I remember his eyes; they blazed like hellfire. I thought he was going to steal my soul. I think he might have?" She sounded confused, "I know a part of me feels like it's missing." She looked down at her left ankle. "Look, he grabbed my ankle." There was a blackened mark wrapped around it and it almost looked like a hand with long nails.

"Lucien, she has a black mark on her ankle. It looks like claw marks. Is it on her body?"

Lucien approached the body and took photos. "Yes, I noticed that. The other bodies have similar marks. Good job, Victoria. Is there anything else that the victim can tell us?"

"She said he was wearing a hood, his eyes burned like they were on fire. Sheila seems certain he tried to take a part of her soul."

Lucien muttered curses under his breath. He pulled out his phone and left the room. I turned back toward Sheila. My eyes roamed over her and noticed the mark on her ankle seemed to darken and lighten as I watched, almost like it was moving.

I touched the mark and froze in shock as the blackness seemed to coil and move up my hand, it felt like I had touched a hot stove and a scream ripped out of me. I watched it coil and twist as it moved up my arm causing shuddering to follow in its wake.

"Victoria?" Lucien ran back into the room, "What's wrong?" He rushed to my side, grasping my shoulders.

"You can't see it?" I cried out as the black mark moved upwards toward my elbow and I tried to push it down with my other hand, which seemed to make it spread and the pain escalated. "Lucien, please help me!"

Lucien cupped my face in his hands. They were warm and that familiar electrical pulse. traveled downward. I could hear him muttering words, but the black mark kept expanding. It was almost to my shoulder.

"Prohibere!" Lucien's hands lit up. Electric tendrils could be seen visibly now as they traveled along my body to my arm and they crashed into the black mark. The pain dulled to an ache and the mark finally stopped moving. I was sobbing by that time and shaking slightly.

"What happened?" Lucien demanded and he tilted my face to look up at him. His eyes roamed my body, looking for what had caused me pain but I could see that he wasn't able to detect the black mark that had transferred from Sheila's ankle to my arm.

Speaking of Sheila, she had uncurled from the corner and was at my right side now. She looked down at her ankle that was now clear of any marks. "You took the blackness away." She sounded as if she couldn't quite believe it. I knew I couldn't. "I feel less tainted." That last part was whispered as she looked into my eyes. "Thank you. I hope you catch him and stop him." She faded.

"I have no idea what just happened." I gulped and sat down staring down at my arm. "Lucien that mark that was on her ankle, I touched it and it moved to me. It hurt; it still does, but whatever spell you cast has dulled it."

Lucien knelt in front of me and took the arm that the mark was on in his hand and when he touched the area, it moved away from his touch, as if afraid of him.

"What you've described sounds like a demon's mark, Victoria. I need you to be very clear and describe to me exactly what it does, looks like, and what it feels like. If it is a demon's mark, you've just discovered what our killer is and you may have just helped us find a way to catch him."

So, I told him everything, in as much detail as I could, and when I told him that it felt like fire, he growled softly. It was a serious situation and I still ached but his growl was sexy as all hell.

"It sounds like a demon's mark. Typically, demons that are contracted or summoned, place them on their intended victims but it sounds like these marks don't occur until after the killer has killed the victims. I don't understand why he would place it after they were dead. You mentioned that Sheila said it felt like a part of her soul was missing?" He paused as I nodded in confirmation. "I'm going to call a colleague at the office who specializes in demon magic and ask about this. I have a theory; I don't want to speculate about it until it's confirmed."

"What about the mark on me? When you touched my arm, it ran away from you."

He grinned. "I'm a wielder of good magic, elemental magic, it stands to reason that my magic hurts it. I've placed a spell on you that will last a few days, at least to stop it from spreading, until we can get more information. You're very pale. Even your lips have become pale. Let's get you home to rest and I'll continue my research tonight. I don't want you alone tonight. Do you have a roommate or someone you can stay with just in case that spell fails and there's someone there to call me?"

"Yes, there's someone who is coming over to my home tonight, I won't be alone."

"Good. Let's get you out of here, you look like you're about to pass out."

I felt like I was going to pass out. It felt like even my bones ached and I could barely keep my eyes open. I was ready to crawl in my bed and sleep.

"Why don't you give me the person's number and I'll call them and make sure they're aware of what to look out for tonight? You should sleep in the car, alright?" His voice was soft and kind, lulling me to sleep even though I was still standing.

I hummed in agreement, mumbling Akira's name to him and handed him my phone as he helped me into the passenger seat. I was asleep before he finished buckling me in.

I'm not sure how long I was asleep for but when my eyes started to pry open, I was laying down, and from the peppermint and lavender smell, I was in my bed. There was a large and very warm body next to me, holding me against a familiar chest that felt like a mini heater.

"Akira?" I blinked up at him, he hadn't been sleeping, he had been reading one of the books from the bookcase across the room. I was curled against his chest as he laid on his side. He placed the book to the side and pulled me closer with the arm that was already wrapped around my middle.

"Hey, V." His voice was soft. "The detective told me what happened. How are you feeling?"

"Better."

And I was. The pain had numbed and I wasn't nearly as exhausted as I had been earlier. I found it strange how I had become so exhausted, even though I had been in pain, so quickly. I wondered if that had anything to do with interacting with the ghosts. It was something to talk to Lucien about. It wasn't like I had ever done what I had done with Tyler and Sheila before. I had never actively touched a ghost and made them corporeal before. It was all sorts of weird with a capital W.

"Good." Akira sat up and pulled me up so that I could rest my back against the headboard. "You're in so much trouble, Vic." He growled; his silver blue eyes flashed. He was actually angry at me.

"Why? I didn't do anything."

"You went along with the detective and got hurt!" His voice rose but I knew he wasn't really mad at me. He was upset about the situation and I smiled at him.

"You're so cute when you get worried. Like a cute lil' angry puffball."

"Puffball?" The indignation on his face was the best part. "Did you just call me, the second in the pack, a puffball?"

"An angry lil' puffball." I nodded happily. "Would it help if I called you my angry puffball?"

"Oh, for fu..." Akira blew out an angry breath before it turned into a low chuckle. "I adore you." He pulled me into his chest again, squeezing me tightly. "Don't worry me like that again, alright?"

I melted. Being held by Akira was probably the best feeling in the world. I was safe with him. His spicy scent was always so soothing and felt like home.

"I'll try? I didn't mean to get a demon mark attached to my arm on purpose."

"If anyone could accidentally do something like that, it would be you." He was teasing yet I knew he was also serious. I sighed in agreement. If anyone could do something as stupid as this, it would be me.

Akira kissed the top of my head, squeezing me tightly to him. "You tell me the second you start feeling any pain again. Got it?"

"Yes, mother."

A frustrated chortle was my answer as he pulled back and shook his head.

"I love you, V. Don't go trying to get yourself hurt, alright?"

Damn this man. He knew just what to do to make me squirm with happiness.

"Yes, yes. No more demon marks. Got it. Can you just kiss me now?" I jutted out my lower lip in a mock pout.

"Oi, you are a brat," Akira thickened his Texan accent and leaned over me, his hand cupping my cheek, running his thumb along my lower lip. I licked his thumb, pulling it into my mouth, biting it. Akira growled again, but this time it was a different kind of growl that sent heat straight between my legs. "Cheeky."

I laughed as he pulled his hand back but he covered my laugh up with his mouth. His tongue dueled with mine for dominance, and his won. I clutched his shoulders, my nails biting into his skin. I moaned softly, sucking on his tongue and was rewarded with another heated growl. Our breath mingled as our kisses became more frantic.

Akira pulled back slightly and I watched as he pulled off his shirt. He was breathtaking in his masculinity. You know how you read in romance novels and the man is hot as sin? Or was so hot panties dropped from young to old? That was Akira. His dark skin just tempted my fingers to explore and a scattering of black hair could be seen above his pants where that deep V begged to be traced and licked. I had looked up what it was called once and it felt fitting to say Akira had an Adonis belt.

I wanted the pants off him immediately. My shirt was thrown off right before I reached out to his belt tugging roughly as he pulled off my pants and panties. It was a hilarious amount of scrambling and clothes pulling. I couldn't help the gasp as the cool air hit my already soaking pussy. I threw his belt across the room, and helped him push his pants down over his hips.

I stared at his cock. It was already standing up and was thicker than the picture I had seen from Lola. A drop of precum was already leaking out of his tip. I had to taste it. I pushed him so that he lay on his back to have easier access to his cock. My head bent over his cock and my lips wrapped around the head. We both moaned as I took his cock into my mouth. He was hard, slick, and his spicy scent filled my mouth.

As I pulled back slightly, my lips trailed his cock as my hands started to stroke him. I hummed as I worked to get his cock fully in my mouth. Akira hissed softly; his hips jerked slightly. He grabbed my hips, pulling my pussy toward him. I felt his fingers brushing along my entrance before two of his fingers pushed inside of me and his thumb pressed against my clit.

I stifled a cry at the sensation and took his cock further into my mouth, sucking it, licking his slit and started to slide my tongue up and down along his hard length. His fingers matched my pace and soon we were both panting as he pushed me to the edge just with his fingers and thumb. I could hear how wet I was as he moved his fingers within me, curling them every time he would thrust in. A warmth exploded and I felt myself shake as I came just from his fingers, I had to pull away from his cock to cry out, stroking his length as I twisted my wrist along his cock, even as I shuddered in early release.

"Baby," Akira's voice was strained, "I'm not going to last if you keep that up."

Akira pulled me away from his cock, kissing me to silence my protest. Our tongues twined together again. I lost all sense of thought as his hands cupped my breasts and he rolled my nipples between his fingers, pinching them roughly. My back arched, pushing them even harder into his hands.

"Akira," I gasped away from his mouth, "stop teasing!" That was my job.

His mouth moved down my neck, sucking and biting in just the right amount of pressure to tear more cries from me. He ignored me as he reached my nipples with his lips. He took my right nipple into his mouth, rolling his tongue around the nipple before his teeth pulled at it while his hand pinched and pulled on my left nipple, stopping just short of painful. My hips jerked upward and my toes were curled as I was lost to his mouth.

I tangled my fingers in his hair and pulled as his mouth moved between my nipples. "Akira!"

"Patience, my love." His voice grumbled. I cried out as his hands moved to my legs, pulling them wide as his mouth continued downward, his tongue dipping over the planes of my stomach. "I'm not even close to being done with you."

"Oh, gods!" I jolted upright as his tongue flicked my clit. His fingers delved into my pussy again, this time with more force and speed. His teeth grazed my clit as he pushed his tongue inside of my pussy along with his fingers that twisted and curled as he moved them in and out. I wasn't going to last long as I felt his tongue flick up toward my clit.

"Ah!" I clutched his head, pulling him closer. I could feel the purr he released as he sucked on my clit and I let out another cry as I came again.

My legs were shaking as Akira pulled back, licking his lips. I watched as he licked and sucked on his fingers that he had used to bring me to another climax. Gods, he was so hot and he knew it.

I reached for him pulling him back down on top of me. I crashed our lips together frantically as my hand moved down and grasped him, squeezing and stroking. He moaned and as his hip thrust in my hand, I knew he had to be inside of me. Akira seemed to have the same mindset because he gently pushed my hand away and pulled my legs around his waist. I could feel his tip brushing along the outside of my pussy and I shuddered.

"I love you." Akira stared into my eyes as he thrust forward, burying himself to his hilt in one stroke.

I cried out at the feeling of his cock inside of me pulsed throughout my body and my hips arched. He slowly pulled out only to thrust back inside of me again. My hips moved to match his thrusts and we were soon moving together as he sped up.

Soon the only sound that could be heard in my studio was our panting mixed with moans. It was just me and him. There was nothing from the outside world that was going to ruin this moment.

I knew he was close when he began to tense under my hands. I whimpered as I felt another release just as he neared his. Akira's breathing became ragged as he pulled out of me and came on my stomach. He held himself over me for several long moments as we both shuddered in the aftermath.

"I love you too." I looked up at him and laughed happily. "That might be a little late to say now." Akira met my eyes and he started to chuckle as well. I went to sit up but he held me down.

"Hold on a second." He got out of the bed, moving to the bath-room door. I heard him turn on the shower then come back to the bed. "Come on, love. Let's get both of us cleaned up." He picked me up under my knees and I wrapped my arms around his neck.

"Oh, such a gentleman." I purred. "Who would have thought?"

"Mmm, just don't tell anyone else." We stepped into the bathroom and spent another hour exploring each other's bodies before the water turned ice cold and we had to hurriedly finish cleaning up and dive back under my beds covers to fall asleep in each other's arms.

CHAPTER 6

*M*y alarm went off a few hours later and I moaned. It was too early to get up, not to mention my body felt used, but in such a good way that I wanted to bask in it. I reached over to shut the alarm off and noticed that my bed was empty. Where was Akira? I sat up, rubbing my eyes as I fought back a yawn.

"And the beauty awakes as the beast finishes making her breakfast." Akira's voice drawled from the kitchen, I looked to the right. He stood at the stove, frying up what smelled like eggs. He had no shirt on and his pants were just barely on, he had left them unbuttoned and zipped. Everything came flooding back.

"Last night wasn't a dream." I breathed out softly.

"I would hope it wasn't a dream. You taste even better than I dreamed." Akira looked over at me with a smirk on his face as my body turned bright red.

"Jerk!" I threw a pillow at him but he caught it before it hit him and tossed it backward, away from the stove.

"Come eat breakfast. You need the energy and nutrients." He turned off the stove and served the eggs onto two plates. "Let's eat together before we have to get moving."

I got out of bed, wrapped a sheet around my body, and went to sit next to him at the bar. We ate breakfast in silence. I ended up leaning against him as we ate. I felt safe and I didn't want it to end. Even the demon mark on my arm couldn't damper this feeling.

"The detective mentioned more work with you today, hopefully he'll have a way to get this mark off of you. I'll drive you to the office since your car is still there and see you later during our shifts?"

"That sounds good." I stood and took the dishes to the sink. "Akira," I was interrupted when Akira's arms wrapped around me from behind. I leaned back into his chest and grinned. "Why do you have a flashlight in your pants?"

"Brat." Akira pulled my face up and we didn't speak for a long while after.

We left my apartment shortly after noon and drove to Lucien's office. The demon mark had begun to ache again and I watched as it began to coil up my arm. I didn't say anything about it to Akira, I didn't want to worry him again. It was enough that I was starting to freak out about it. Akira dropped me off in front of Lucien's office before heading off to the bar to get the prep work done.

The kappa receptionist waved me right through and I went into Lucien's office as the door was open. I knocked on the door anyway when I stepped in. Lucien was behind his desk and another man sat across from him.

"Oh, the receptionist didn't say you had someone in here, I'm sorry." I turned around to go wait outside of the office but Lucien called me back.

"Victoria, I would like you to meet my co-worker, Shane. He's a shaman and has some knowledge about demon marks."

I stopped and blinked at the man who turned in his seat to look at me. He was an older man with dark skin and no hair on his head, he had wrinkles around his eyes and a massive beard. He smiled at me, his teeth flashing against his dark skin.

"Shane the Shaman? Your parents must have hated you."

Lucien balked and I slapped my hand over my mouth. I hadn't meant to say that out loud.

Shane didn't seem fazed by my observation though. He let out a loud laugh and slapped his knee. "Oh, I like this one, Lucien." His voice almost sounded like sandpaper against wood. "No, my parents loved me very much but they weren't the smartest in the shed." He winked at me. I sat next to him and took his hand. "It's a pleasure to meet you, my dear."

"I told Shane about yesterday's events with the ghosts and what you described when you touched the ghost's ankle."

"Yes," Shane leaned back in his chair and I noticed that he wasn't very tall maybe only an inch or two taller than I was, "it's an interesting situation. Not to mention how you interact with the dead. I work with the Spirit Elemental but interacting with her is much different from how you interact with the ghosts. At least from what Lucien has told me." He laced his fingers together. "I serve the elements and they seem concerned about the shifting of power this killer could bring to the world."

"Well, if the killer is a demon, doesn't that mean he would have been summoned by someone? I've never heard of a full blooded demon being able to manifest on Earth alone in centuries."

Shane made a surprised sound. "That's correct. I am surprised you know this but I shouldn't be. You are a Dwight, after all. If it truly is a demon, then someone did summon him and that person will be close by when he kills." Shane placed a bag on Lucien's desk and pulled out a few random things, one of which was a long drumstick, his shaman's wand. "I think I can help you with both issues. But first, let's get that demon mark off of you." He turned toward me and held out his hand. "May I see your arm?"

I glanced between Shane and Lucien. I didn't know Shane from Suzy on the corner but I trusted Lucien. Lucien nodded at me.

"He can be trusted. He was a mentor of mine years ago. He was the one who saved me from the troll." He smiled gently. "I wouldn't entrust your safety to someone I didn't trust."

Oh, he had a cute smile that probably led all the females to his bed with just a twist of his lips.

I placed my arm on the table and pointed to where the demon taint coiled near my elbow. "It keeps moving more toward my shoulder. The spell that Lucien cast last night seemed to stop the pain for a few hours, it's still only a little bit painful right now, and it briefly stopped moving during the night."

Shane lifted my arm, peering closely at it and moved it up and down. "It's strange. I can't see the mark, same as Lucien, but I can sense the taint." Unlike when Lucien touched my arm and the mark avoided his touch, when Shane touched the mark, I could feel it trying to leave my arm and attach to him. "You did a good job stopping it in its tracks, Lucien. Not many can stop demon taint once it takes a hold of its victim."

"It's trying to jump to you." I pulled my arm back and the demon taint's pain throbbed, I couldn't hold back my wince this time.

"It won't want to do that if it knew how I was going to get rid of it." Shane's voice was serious and I looked over at him as he started to pull more things from his bag. He placed several crystal-like objects on the desk in a circle, along with a small tape recorder. "Now," he moved in the chair so that he was facing me, "I am going to call on Spirit and she will assist in purging the demon taint. It is going to hurt, but I believe if Lucien casts the spell he did previously before we start, it will lessen the pain."

Lucien nodded and stood from his chair and came to stand next to me. He placed his hand on my arm and as it warmed under his touch, the electric sensation caused a small shiver down my spine. He whispered his spell again and the pain that had been steadily coming back now dulled again.

I sighed and nodded up at him. "Thanks." When I was with Akira, I hadn't noticed the pain.

"Oh, this should be good." Siobal appeared next to me suddenly like a rabbit. "I always loved how shamans worked." She looked down at my arm sadly. "I'm sorry you got infected. Let the shaman know that I want to help."

"Siobal is here and she wants to help." I looked up at both of them.

"Lucien told me about Siobal. I will pray for her peace and if she can offer assistance, what idea does she have to assist us?"

I looked at Siobal and I repeated her words as she spoke. That wasn't weird at all.

"If Spirit allows, I would like to offer some of my power to Victoria. It won't be my full power, that is gone now, but it will help her in times of great peril by offering her a warning."

I paused and my eyes widened. "Siobal, I can't let you do that."

"Why not? I don't have any use for my powers since I'm dead." Her answer was dry and very sarcastic. I winced; I had walked right into that one. "Besides, it might not be much."

"I think if Siobal is wanting to help us, you should allow it." Shane muttered thoughtfully. "I don't feel any negative energy from Spirit, so she will most likely help. Let us begin."

Shane pressed a button on the tape recorder and the sound of drums filled the room. He held his wand over his knee and started to move it in time with the beat. "I'm going to go into a trance. Victoria, if you will relax, as best as you can, and close your eyes and focus on the drum beats. And Siobal, you will know what to do when the time comes." He closed his eyes and I could hear a faint humming from him that matched the drum beats as he started to sway.

I followed his directions by closing my eyes and I found myself humming along with the drum beats. The dull ache from the demon taint throbbed but soon all I could hear and feel was the recording of the drums. The beat sped up after a few minutes and I started to open my eyes. They flew open after a moment as I got a better look at

Shane. He was glowing as he swayed back and forth humming to the beat of the drums as he beat his wand on his knee.

The glow seemed to emit from inside of him and get brighter. The drums stopped suddenly for ten beats. Shane's eyes opened, his pupils and irises were white. He stopped moving his wand as the drums started up again.

"Child," the voice that came from Shane's mouth was a woman's that sounded almost ethereal, "my shaman asks that I help you and I have agreed. A demon that is hell-bent on killing people and exposing the supernaturals to the human world must be stopped." Shane's face moved slightly to look at Siobal standing beside me. "But first, take the girls hand and focus on your will as she focuses on transferring her power to you." His gaze went back to me. "Child, focus on Siobal's desire to help you."

I held my hand up to Siobal and she took it in hers. Like before, I was able to touch her as if she were actually there. Her hand was cool as she squeezed mine. She gave me a small smile, it was the first time she looked sincere and I smiled back. An eerie noise filled the room and the light seemed to dim until only the glow from Shane was visible.

"Focus, child." The woman's voice was stern and jeered me back to looking at my hand and Siobal's.

She had said to focus on Siobal's desire to help so I closed my eyes again and concentrated on my desire to help her as well, to let her rest in peace by catching her killer.

Our hands felt like they were warming up as the drums continued in the background. I could hear the woman's voice and Siobal was humming along so I started humming again. Soon our hands warmed even more and I felt that warmth spread up toward my chest. I heard a soft exclamation of awe from Lucien and I opened my eyes to look over at him. He was staring at me as if I had sprouted a second head.

I tilted my head at him before blinking and looked down at

Siobal's and my hand. That same glow that emitted from Shane as Spirit possessed him, was now coming from me. My mouth dropped and I glanced between us. Siobal smirked at me and wiggled her fingers at me with her other hand. The drum recording suddenly lessened, the beat happening every ten seconds now. I looked over at Shane.

His eyes were still white as he stopped humming. "Siobal, do you freely give what you can of your powers to this child?"

"I, Siobal The Seer, do freely give what powers I can to Victoria Dwight." Siobal's voice was serious and as she finished speaking there was a loud clap from the tape recorder, as if a large clap of thunder was recorded. A jolt of energy ran through our hands and up to my chest. I blinked as my skin glowed brighter for several seconds before the glow disappeared.

"I'll see you later." Siobal let go of my hand and started to disappear. "I need to rest. I'll visit you soon and we can explore what powers Spirit was able to transfer to you. Good luck."

"Now, child," Shane's voice now sounded like his and Spirits together, "let's take care of the darkness that afflicts you." He leaned forward and the end of his wand touched the arm with the demon taint.

The demon taint moved rapidly on my arm, trying to get away from the end of the wand but Shane moved it over the arm rapidly. Spirits voice cracked out and the walls seemed to shake. "Release dispergeret!"

Wind flew through the room, causing books and paperwork to fly across the room. The lights started to flicker on again. I whimpered as I felt the demon taint rage against the spell that was just cast. Spirit continued to chant the spell, each time she repeated it, it echoed and bounce off the walls over and over again. Shane reached out and grasped my arm, forming his hand into a claw, and the demon taint came off my arm, writhing in Shane's hand so much that it looked like a snake.

"So that's demon taint." Lucien muttered, still standing next to me. "I've never seen it active before." His hands come to rest on my shoulders. "You're looking better already." His voice is low as we both watched as Shane crushed the demon taint in his hand before throwing the writhing shadow into his mouth.

"What the heck!" Did that really just happen?

The wind died down and the drums came to a stop, the tape recorder turned itself off. Shane's eyes returned to normal and he stopped glowing. A large burp emitted from him as he started putting the crystals back into his bag.

"Mmm, I've never had demon taint before. Tastes a little like a burnt hotdog."

"You ATE the demon taint?" I sputtered. That was a little gross. Okay, maybe a lot gross.

Shane laughed another belly laugh and zipped up his bag. "Correction," he winked at me, "Spirit ate the demon taint and I was just the vessel. I get the benefits of a full belly though." He patted his stomach and laughed again.

"How are you feeling?" Lucien squeezed my shoulders. I looked up and got caught for a few moments staring into his brown eyes, the gold around his irises seemed to be glowing. "Victoria?" His brows creased in worry when I didn't respond.

"Oh," I snapped out of it and looked away from him, "I'm feeling a lot better."

And I was feeling better. There was no more pain in my arm and that draining feeling I had been feeling since this whole thing had begun had lessened. I was almost feeling like my normal self. I looked back to Shane.

"What did you do? You didn't just remove the demon taint, did you?"

"Mm. You are a smart cookie, aren't you? You shouldn't let your mother push you around." He covered his mouth as he yawned. "Sorry, channeling one of the elements is always exhausting." He shook his head. "But to answer your question, no, Spirit did not just remove the demon taint from you. When Siobal passed you a tiny bit of her power so that you can be warned of danger, Spirit gifted you a small piece of herself as well. With her power, the drain on your life energy that was happening before, is no longer a concern. You can support Siobal on this plane without worry to your life. The elements aren't known for their generosity, so she must have seen something in you to pass on such a gift."

I had been told my whole life by my mother and younger brother that I was weird and there was nothing special, or unique, about me. Now, even though the circumstances that caused it was horrible, within the past few days, I had strangers tell me that I should be proud of my dud powers.

Lucien was the first person outside of my family and pack who believed in me. I always told myself that I was ok with being able to communicate with ghosts and not have any powers like mom or be a shifter like my brother and dad but, deep down, it always hurt that I was the black sheep of the family.

"She's always had it within her, Shane. It seems like she just needed a push." Lucien chuckled at Shane and interrupted my thought process. "I'm not surprised the elements agreed."

Shane stood, took my hand and made a low bow, causing my own laughter to bubble out. "It was a true pleasure, Victoria. Have Lucien give me a ring if you ever need my assistance again." With a kiss to my knuckles he swept out of the room with an imaginary cloak causing me to laugh again.

"I like him. I thought shamans were scary."

Lucien moved over to the other side of the desk and sat in his chair. "Don't mistake his jovial attitude. He can be plenty scary when the situation calls for it. I have to say I'm surprised he assisted us so easily."

"You are?" I thought that Shane seemed like the kind of person to offer his shirt to someone in need, at least that's the sense I got from him anyway.

"Mmm, he's a wonderful person over all but his power is granted from the elements and for one of them to work directly through him is a big deal." He was putting paperwork back in stacks on his desk, not that the wind from before had made the office look any messier than it already had.

"But I am glad he helped with Spirit. Not to mention the power transfer from Siobal and Spirit. Now," he focused on me, "you're probably worn out. Why don't you head home and get a few hours of rest before your shift? We can pick up tomorrow by going to Siobal's house?

"Alright, detective, let's go clue hunting tomorrow. It's a date. What are you hoping to find?"

"Honestly," Lucien ran a hand through his hair, the tousled hair look was pretty distracting, "anything at this point. She's the first victim that the killer didn't get to complete his normal M.O. on. I think that would frustrate him. He stalked her differently from the others. He had to know that where he killed her, and when, would be discovered almost instantly. She was a powerful seer. Her house was protected by powerful wards. My team say that when they went into the home, none of the wards were active. He went there searching for something, her death was just a distraction, at least that's my theory. We weren't able to find what, but maybe you can find out from Siobal if something is missing. I have a gut feeling, I'm not often wrong." He didn't even look fazed by the date comment.

I snorted, "Cocky, much?"

"You have no idea. Comes with the territory."

"Which one? Being a wizard or a detective?"

"Both." He smirked at me as he walked me out to my car.

We said goodbye and I left to take a nap before I started my shift at eight. I would think about what happened and these powers that I apparently had been gifted later. When I wouldn't have a meltdown like a crazy person.

I walked into the bar thirty minutes before my shift. Uncle Ray was behind the bar rearranging the top shelf spirits by color. He knew I hated that.

"Really, Uncle Ray?" I laughed sitting on a barstool. "You know I'll change it right back when I clock in, right?"

"You really should leave it the way I put it." He grumbled as he turned toward me. "I'm the owner and I could fire you, you know that?"

He always said that but we both knew he was full of hot air. I respected him as the alpha of the pack but he was still my uncle who I went to for pretty much everything since I was old enough to recognize how toxic my mother and brother were. My father was usually too busy with his pack to pay any attention so my uncle stepped up when he could.

"I love you too." I leaned over and kissed his cheek. "Any news?"

Uncle Ray picked up a clean rag and started to wipe the corner of the bar where my signature was. "I've had the pack rotating patrols. We can't find any scent of this guy. That detective even let me send Sean and Chase to look for his scent at the other crime scenes, but everything is too old to get a solid lead." If you didn't know him, he was the perfect picture of nonchalance. He was anything but. I would not want to be the killer if Uncle Ray caught him before Detective Lucien did.

"Well, hopefully Detective Lucien will find him soon." I grabbed the rag from Uncle Ray and hopped off the stool. "Where's Akira?" I joined him behind the bar and started to reorganize the alcohol that he had just moved.

"You don't even wait until I am out of sight?" Uncle Ray growled before he held me in his grip as he tickled my sides. I squeaked and tried to get away but ended up giving up and yelling out that I surrendered. "Akira is just starting the third patrol so he'll be done around closing time."

"Ah." I wondered if Akira had had time to talk to Uncle Ray

about us. He had to have noticed our scents together but he could just be waiting for one of us to say something. "Hey, Uncle Ray..."

Just then one of the pack came in, just getting off patrol in wolf form. They were large, almost as tall as some horses and nearly as wide. They shared most physical features with normal wolves, just much larger and their front legs were thicker than the back ones. Even a small werewolf could easily take down a grown grizzly. Most people would scream the second they set their eyes on a werewolf if it weren't for a glamour all shifters possessed. Most humans either didn't notice them or thought they saw something else.

Uncle Ray mussed my hair and went over to the wolf. "We'll catch up later, alright?" He looked over his shoulder at me and winked. "Have fun reorganizing."

Reorganizing the bottles on the bar shelves took longer than I had anticipated because we had a rush of customers throughout the night. Most were regulars but there was a sense of tense desperation in the air as more folks discussed Siobal's and the other murders. Everyone was on edge, wondering if a loved one or they themselves would be next.

I hadn't heard from Lola since we had texted earlier but that wasn't unusual. Working at the law firm usually kept her pretty busy, sometimes having to work 24 hours to prepare for a case. I still wanted to tell her about Akira, it would just be better face to face rather than text.

"Hey, blondie!" I sighed and internally rolled my eyes as I faced the familiar and irritating regular. You guessed it, Carl the nasty gnome. "I want a screwdriver!" Carl had parked himself on the middle bar stool.

I narrowed my eyes at him. "Pay upfront." I wasn't going to deal with his attitude tonight.

"Yeah, yeah, just hurry it up." Carl handed me a ten.

I rang up his drink, handed him his change, and started making the screwdriver. It took less than a minute to make with just some vodka and orange juice in a tall glass. I added an orange slice and slid the glass to him. "One screwdriver."

"Thanks, blondie!" He looked around the bar behind him. "What's with the doom and gloom?"

I sighed as I placed the vodka back on the shelf. "You haven't heard about the killing near here"

"Oh," Carl almost gulped the whole drink down in one swallow, "who cares about some idiot getting killed?"

Rage flashed through me as I rounded on him. "Idiot? How dare you! Someone died! A living person who had their life taken from them in a senseless death." I had to resist the urge to throw an empty glass at his ugly mug.

"Cool your jets," Carl grumbled and finished his drink. "Friggin' crazy ass bitch."

"Alright. That's it!" I grabbed his glass and thunked it into the sink under the bar. "GET OUT!" I raised my voice and motioned with my head for Uncle Ray who was making his way back to the bar when he heard my voice rise. "You're banned from the bar until you learn some manners, you sad excuse of an imitation garden gnome." I was ready to rip his throat out.

"What? I've been coming here for over thirty years! You don't get to treat me this way!" Carl stood on the stool and looked about ready to lunge at me.

"That's enough of that." Uncle Ray grabbed the back of his shirt. "It's time for you to leave. Maybe we'll let you back after you've learned some manners like my niece has suggested." He pulled Carl up so that he was face to face and his teeth lengthened as he growled softly. "If you ever speak that way to my niece again, you'll go missing. Understood?"

He didn't wait for a reply as he threw Carl toward the door. Chase was there to catch Carl and help him none to gently out the door into the street. The sound of Carl's enraged snarling was cut short as Chase slammed the door and wiped his hands.

Good riddance. There weren't many things that got under my skin, being called a bitch was the last straw. Uncle Ray let me clock out early and I sent a text to Akira letting him know I would see him tomorrow.

CHAPTER 7

I had gotten an early start to my day all gung ho to get started but Lucien had been busy until almost five in the afternoon. It was lucky I had the night off. When I had met him at his office, he had looked disheveled and stressed. I had insisted on some coffee before we got in his car.

Siobal's apartment was more like a townhouse. It was located in a gated neighborhood. The security guard hadn't wanted to let us in, even when Lucien showed him a badge that looked like a human detectives. Maybe he had run ins with cops before and was holding a grudge. Or he was an idiot. Or both. Lucien became impatient while he waited on the guard to decide if he was going to let us in that he waved his hand at the man, a light emitting from his palm. After he did that, the man slumped in his chair. Lucien got out of the car, pressed the gate button and we went through.

"He'll wake up in a few minutes feeling more refreshed than he has in a long time." Lucien promised as we drove through the neighborhood. "It's the spell I used on you before I dropped you off at your home the other night." That explained how I was able to have the energy of a bunny with Akira in the sheets later on.

"You're kind of adorable with how impatient you are." I laughed but almost choked a second afterward when I realized what I had said. Why did hanging out with this man make me feel like I do when I'm with Akira, warm and safe and a bad habit of saying stupid things?

He grinned at me, and I swear to the gods, a dimple appeared in his right cheek. Dimples were my weakness. Along with muscular biceps that I could sink my teeth into. Oh, and abs, couldn't forget those.

"Adorable, huh? I have to say, no one has called me that before."

"Don't let it go to your head." I mumbled as we pulled in front of a modern looking townhome, it was the only one that was painted bright red. "I wonder how she got away with that with her HOA." I climbed out of the car, closing the door shut.

"I had a witch cast a spell on the HOA members. Anytime they get a complaint it mysteriously disappeared." Siobal was next to Lucien as she looked up at the townhome with pride. "This was my home; I think it's what I will miss the most."

"You came." I looked at her and smiled. "I didn't know if you would after yesterday. I was afraid you'd drained yourself too much." I was getting used to ghosts just appearing when they were being talked about around me now. I never noticed the pattern before. I hadn't cared to.

"You can call me anytime, I'll come. The detective is right to check my apartment though. I sense that the one who killed me has been inside recently. Probably before and after the MEPA came and went."

I told Lucien what she said and he snapped into professional mode. "Stay behind me and if I say to run, you run. Got it?" He left his hands loose, a wizard had no need for a gun, and he opened the door.

Inside it was sparsely furnished and everything was white. I looked at Siobal and raised an eyebrow. "Really? White?"

She shrugged. "I like my colors bright outside and neutral inside.

It helped my visions. Don't ask." She flew past Lucien through the living area and up the spiral stairs. "He was in my bedroom."

Lucien went through the house, placing wards around the house, and he seemed angry. "Either my crew forgot to ward this house, which is unlikely, or our killer is capable of neutralizing wards."

"Well, that sucks."

He looked at me, his eyes showing a rage that he held in check. "It sucks majorly."

I followed him up the stairs that turned into a large loft area. Siobal floated in front of a vanity on the other side of the room.

"He took my summoning crystal. Tell the detective that it was a class four summoning crystal and could be worn as a necklace."

When I told Lucien this information, he decorated the walls blue with his language. I had to say I was impressed; I didn't think he had that kind of pirate language in him.

"I take it a summoning crystal is a big deal?" I should probably know this from all of my mother's lessons but I was never really interested in magic that relied on rocks like mom was. It was just one of the ways I tried to rebel against her.

"Yes," Lucien spoke before Siobal, "summoning crystals are in five classes. One is the weakest while five is the strongest." He started digging through the vanity.

"I used the summoning crystal to focus my energy and to store my magical energy when I was saving up for a vision, I knew I would use a lot. It held almost a third of my power inside of it. And the killer can now access that." She looked worried for the first time. "I was a very powerful clairvoyant, Vickie. If he uses my magic, he could use it to find victims with a lot of magic if he knows how or avoid the detective indefinitely."

"Well, fudgesicles." I winced. "That's not good. Isn't there anything we can do to track the crystal?"

She shook her head. "No, it was keyed to me and if I were alive, I could track it." She went over to her dresser and looked at the pictures on top. "But, maybe," She looked up at me, "because you have a little bit of my power now, you might be able to find it."

"Uh, what? Is that even possible?" I stared at her dumbly.

"Is what possible?" Lucien walked over to me.

"Siobal thinks with the power she gave me I could find the crystal. Is such a thing possible?"

Lucien's brow was furrowed as he thought for several minutes in silence.

"I'm willing to try anything at this point. I want this demon caught. What does Siobal propose that you do?"

"You need to channel your power, build it up. I focused on my question, or what I wanted to know and it came to me after I powered enough energy."

"Well, how do I gain that energy?"

Siobal shrugged. "I did it through sex. I doubt that would work for you, unless you want to test it with Mr. Sexywizard here."

"I doubt having sex with Lucien, even if it would be mind-blowing, would help with this situation where I need to gain magical energy."

It only took a second to see Siobal smirk to notice that Lucien, who had wandered over to the vanity again, stiffen and look back at me. I had said that loud enough so that he heard it. I groaned and covered my face with my hands.

"Not that I'm not flattered," Lucien's voice, full of amusement, cut through my groan, "I think I might have an idea on how to help you focus and build your magical energy."

I cleared my throat and choose to ignore the fact I had just told Lucien I wanted to have sex with him. I was going to ignore that happened. Yep. Ignore it. "What's that?"

"Remember how you meditated and were able to call Siobal's ghost? I think if we drew a circle around you and you meditated, the energy would build within the circle and would only have one place to go and that would be to you."

Siobal nodded, although she was still laughing at me. "That will probably work."

"Sure, let's do that." Anything to get my face to go back to its normal shade of color and not red.

"Let's go downstairs, Siobal's kitchen has cement flooring. That will give us a good place to make the circle without any interference." Lucien was being kind not to suggest using Siobals bedroom because that would have been awkward and rude since she was here.

We had just started toward the stairs when there was a loud boom, the house shook, and Siobal screamed.

"He's here!"

"Get down!" Lucien pushed me to the ground and a blue energy field generated over our heads as he kneeled next to me. "Someone has breached my wards."

"Siobal says it's the killer." I squeaked out as another large boom generated from downstairs and I clutched onto one of Lucien's arms.

"Shit." He moved his arms in front of him, drawing symbols quickly in the air, his metal fingers glowing a bright yellow, "He's destroying my wards faster than I can put them up." He looked down at me. "I'm going to draw him away, I need you to get into the car and get out of here. There's a cell phone in the console, call the contact labeled MQ and tell him what's happening."

I gaped at him. "I'm not leaving you here!"

"And what good will you be?" Siobal appeared in front of me. "He's a high level wizard for the god's sake. Can you cast offensive magic?"

I jerked back and shook my head. "No, I can't."

Lucien grabbed both of my arms and looked down at me. "I'll be fine. You need to get out of here. Run down the stairs after you count to ten, got it?"

I nodded. "Please be careful."

His grin was cocky again. "I'll kick his ass," he disappeared down the stairs and I started counting.

At ten I raced down the stairs, clinging to the rails as more shocks and booms sounded from downstairs, Lucien was giving as good as the killer was. I barely managed to dodge a piece of wood that flew by my head and I basically crawled on my hands and knees toward the door.

"Drop down!" Siobal appeared in front of me and I did as she instructed just as a red energy ball zoomed past and blew apart the front door. "He's after you." Siobal sounded shocked. "He's after you, Vickie. Get up, run!"

I scrambled to my feet, I didn't have to be told twice, and ran outside, trying to stay upright. I got to the driver's side of the car when I looked back in time to watch Lucien fly through the entrance and hit the pavement, skidding across it. He was bleeding from his forehead and cuts all along his body. He grunted as he sat up, his left arm hung limply at his side as he threw out his right one and lightning streaked from his hand inside of the house.

I watched as the lightning hit a tall figure in a black cloak, throwing them backward into the house. I ran over to Lucien, grabbing his right arm, helping him stand.

"Victoria, you need to get in the car and go." He growled out, "He's after you, for some reason."

"Not without you, detective." I opened the passenger door and pushed him, not so gently, into the car, slamming the door. "Buckle up." ·

I ran to the driver side just as the figure appeared through the rubble. I watched in horror, even as I dived into the drivers' seat, as a clawed hand with black nails reached upward and another ball of red energy was thrown at us. Lucien shouted a word and a gust of wind, more like a mini daredevil, hit the red ball and it flew up into the air.

"Go!" Lucien yelled out at me as I turned on the car and slammed on the pedal in reverse as he threw another wind spell to knock down the killer.

We got around the block before I was able to throw the car in a U-turn and move it into drive. The car flew through the gated community entrance, just barely scraping through the gate that had been closing behind another car. I had to drive up onto the sidewalk to avoid running into the back of the car in front of us.

"Lucien, you're really hurt. We need to go to the hospital." I turned right onto the road and ignored the speed limit hoping we didn't run into any human police. I wasn't going to let this man die for protecting me.

"No," Lucien grunted as he opened up his glove box and pulled out a small bag that was filled with tiny vials that had some type of liquid in them. "I'll have one of these and be fine. I need you to take us to your uncle's bar while I call my boss."

"Why the bar?" I slowed down after we had gotten far enough away for my peace of mind. I looked at Lucien out of the corner of my eye as he swallowed two vials and placed the bag back into the glove box.

"Your uncle's pack is there, or at least enough, that will be a deterrent to this killer, until I can regroup and formulate a plan." He winced as he pulled his seat belt on, his arm still not working yet but the scratches starting to close. "He went after you, basically bulldozed over me to get at you." He looked over at me. "I want to know why."

"You and me both." We were on the highway now, headed to Gilbert and fighting traffic to get over to the HOV lane. "Siobal yelled at me that he was aiming at me. If it weren't for her, one of those spells would have gotten me in the back." I couldn't stop the shudder that went through me.

"I think," Lucien moaned as he moved his arm, "I think you might be his next target."

I almost drove us into the median before righting the car. "What?!" I stuttered, "Why in the world would I be a target?"

"That's the question, isn't it?" Lucien's voice was soft but he placed his hand on my thigh with his good one and squeezed, "I'll protect you."

And if that statement and touch didn't send hot shivers down my stomach to pool between my legs, I'd be the Easter bunny hyped up on candy.

---

*W*hen we walked through Supe's Karaoke Bar, Uncle Ray was behind the bar with Akira. My throat tightened and I rushed inside.

"Akira?" He had turned around when we had come in and met me halfway, pulling me close after he got a look at my face.

"What happened?" Uncle Ray's authoritative voice rang out through the empty bar. "You're covered in blood."

"We ran into the killer while your niece was assisting me." Lucien sat at the bar as Akira, who had picked me up and placed me on a bar stool, glared at him.

"What do you mean, you ran into the killer?"

I placed my hand on one of Akira's and squeezed. "We were looking at Siobals home when he broke in. If it weren't for Lucien, I would have died." I leaned into his side and tried to relax, exhaustion seeping through me now that my adrenaline was wearing off. "It's not his fault, I offered to help. Don't be angry at him, please."

Uncle Ray glanced between Akira and I and I noticed that he jerked his head at Akira and when our eyes met, he glared. Uh oh. Cat was out of the bag, and it seemed he wasn't happy. Maybe he hadn't noticed our scents together.

"Ray, I think the killer has decided that Victoria is his next victim."

I watched in fascination as Uncle Ray fought himself for control, his hands already transformed into his wolf's claws. A low and angry growl fought its way out of his chest. Lucien held up his hands even as he winced in pain. "I have called in for assistance but, let's be honest, she will be safer, if she's with either myself, or one of your wolves, until I can catch him. I would prefer if she was with me and one of your wolves as back up, if possible." He looked at Uncle Ray with respect but kept his face serious and unwavering.

"I don't want the pack in danger just because some lunatic took a liking to me." I glance between the two.

"Shush. You're family, niece." Uncle Ray growled out at me and my mouth shut quickly. "Akira, you and I need to talk but I want you with these two until the issue is resolved. And you," he glanced over at Lucien, "I will allow my second to help you in this, but his first duty is her safety." He focused on me next. "I want to talk to you in my office now. Akira, get the detective something to drink." Uncle Ray walked around the bar and headed to the stairs, I followed with my head down. I felt like I had just gotten caught with my hand in the cookie jar. Heh. Akira was quite the cookie.

I decided that being quiet and waiting to see what Uncle Ray said was probably the best bet instead of diving in half-cocked. My hands were clenched in front of me as we entered his office and sat down. I'm pretty sure I was going to cry later tonight but I held it back for now.

"Vickie," Uncle Ray's voice was soft, "would you look at me?"

I looked up and met his eyes. They were filled with love and concern. My shoulders relaxed. I shouldn't have worried. Uncle Ray wasn't mom.

"So, we have a few things to talk about. Let's start with this killer. How did you get so involved?"

I sighed and proceeded to tell him about what had been happening, starting when Lucien had encouraged me to summon Siobal's ghost, even though he knew most of it. Uncle Ray stayed quiet throughout my story and only interrupted once to pour us some water.

"So," he grinned, "your powers are evolving and you can now give your mother the middle finger." He chuckled as I laughed. "Out of this crazy situation, it looks like some good has happened." He sobered. "When were you going to tell me about you and Akira? I suspected but I would have liked to be told."

"Ah," I scratched the back of my head, "You know that I've always had feelings for him and the other night I told him. Turns out, he feels the same way. He was going to talk to you but it sounds like you've been really busy with pack business."

Uncle Ray laughed, a big barrel laugh that shook his shoulders, "Oh, Vickie, I love you, girl, but you are pretty dense. I've known Akira has been in love with you since he first came here. I'm just surprised how long this has taken. He's a good man and I'll be happy when he takes over as Alpha when I retire. I'll be interested to see how it goes between the detective and Akira as they guard you. That detective seems to have taken a liking to you as well." He reached across the table and took my hands. "As far as this killer goes, I'm sending out the pack and we're going hunting until this killer is found and taken care of."

"Uncle Ray, this guy is scary powerful. Lucien is a high level wizard, I saw the kinds of magic he threw, and this killer just brushed off his spells like he was a fly. The pack won't stand a chance!"

"Now, Vic," Uncle Ray stood up and he was flexing his hands again, "we are more powerful than you give us credit for. We are going to hunt this killer with your detective and we will stop him from hurting you. I'll keep the bar closed until we figure things out, and don't you worry about your paycheck, you'll still have it."

I sighed as I flopped my head and arms on the desk. Uncle Ray was more stubborn than a werebear guarding their donuts. Uncle Ray walked around the desk and pulled me up into his arms, my feet dangled in the air as he hugged me tightly.

"I won't have my niece threatened. You are my family."

"I love you too, Uncle Ray." I smiled into his chest and hugged him back.

When we walked down the stairs, I could hear the soft murmurs of conversation. It sounded like more people had come into the bar, most likely more pack. I saw Chase, with his lemon bright hair, sitting at one of the tables with his boyfriend, Sean who was the packs third, and he waved at me. Akira was behind the bar again and was standing in front of Lucien with his arms crossed. Lucien was looking better; I think the vials he had earlier must have kicked in. I hoped his arm was better, that had looked painful.

I slid into the seat next to him. "Hi guys."

Akira smiled at me softly and passed me a glass of whiskey. "Drink it." He chuckled as I stuck my tongue out at him and chugged the whiskey, coughing as it went down.

"You know you're supposed to sip that." Lucien had his own glass and took a sip to show me how it was done. "Like that." Sarcastic ass.

But suddenly tears started flowing, even though I laughed at his joke, and I tried to stop them but they just decided they were coming out and I had no say. My chest was warm from the alcohol and I finally felt safe after the attack. I hadn't even noticed how scared I had been up until now, maybe now that the adrenaline finally wore off, my body was ready to give in to the tears.

A warm arm wrapped around my shoulder, pulling me against a hard, but comforting, body. I smiled up wobbly at Lucien and was about to thank him when another arm wrapped around my shoulder from the other side, draping over Lucien's. I looked over and Akira was on my other side but he was looking at Lucien. Mr. Angry Puff-ball was feeling territorial and I wasn't sure if that made me happy or annoyed, considering I liked Lucien as well. Lucien winked at Akira and I watched Akira fight a smile.

"We agreed that it would be good to stay at Detective Lucien's house." Akira glanced down at me after a few more seconds of eye tag with Lucien. "I have some clothes in the back and we'll pick up some clothes from your apartment."

"Ok, I guess. I know my apartment wouldn't have enough room for all three of us. We'd end up laying on top of each other and I'm not sure my AC could handle all the male hotness."

And there went my mouth again and the steam out of my ears. I grabbed the remains of Lucien's whiskey and swallowed it. Lucien was chuckling softly and Akira looked at me amused.

Alright, time to avoid that topic. "Could we head out soon? I'm feeling really tired." Which was true, I could feel the exhaustion starting to seep through even more.

Akira nodded. "Yeah, let me tell Ray, and we'll head out with the detective."

I stifled a yawn as Lucien looked concerned at me as his eyes roamed over my face.

"You're pale again, you can sleep on the way to my place."

I yawned this time and nodded. "I think sleep sounds like an amazing idea."

"When we get in the car, I'll cast that spell on you so you can get some sleep." He helped me stand as Akira rounded the bar. "Let's get your things and get to my place."

I rode in the backseat since Akira was taller and he would have been uncomfortable in the backseat. As I buckled in, Lucien opened the door and placed his palm on my forehead. The last thing I saw was his face as I fell unconscious.

"She should be waking soon. I used a sleep spell on her, along with an additional energy spell, but I doubt she'll be a hundred percent. She'll need to sleep more tonight." Lucien's voice filtered through the fog that was clearing in my head. My head felt heavy but, surprisingly, I wasn't feeling as exhausted as I had been. I opened my eyes, blinking at a ceiling that was covered in stick on glow in the dark stars. I was definitely not in my studio.

"Stars?" My voice came out like a frog croak and that made me giggle, which sounded even worse.

"Vic," the bed dipped and Akira's face appeared before mine, blocking out the stars on the ceiling. "Hey, baby." He grinned. "You've been asleep about two hours. It's a little after three a.m. We picked up clothes and are at Lucien's now." He leaned down and pressed his lips to mine and I wrapped my arms around his neck.

"Mmm," I sigh happily as he pulled back, "a girl could get used to that." I pulled myself up using his arm and glanced around. "This is Lucien's home? This bedroom is the size of two studio apartments and this bed, "I blushed, "it has to be bigger than a king, right? Who needs that?"

A low chuckle came from my other side as Lucien sat on the other end of the bed. "I like a big bed. It was custom made." He had changed from his suit into jeans and a black t-shirt that seemed to be a second skin on him. "Akira and I went around my home, reinforced my wards with both of our blood. You're safe for tonight. It's easier to protect you if we're both in the same room." He handed me a glass of water that I sipped on. I glanced between the two of them.

"Thank you. So, if this is your room, Lucien, what's with the stickers?" I pointed upwards.

Akira started laughing as Lucien groaned. "Told you she would ask as soon as she was up. I win. Pay up." He held out his hand as Lucien grumbled and pulled out his wallet, handing him two twenties.

"You two made a bet how I would react to the stars?"

They both, at least, looked a little guilty before laughing again.

"To answer your question, my nephew put those up there a few years ago before my sister moved away and I can't bring myself to take them down." There was a slight sense of sadness when he mentioned his sister and nephew. "I know, they are kind of childish, but when it's dark, I actually enjoy them. I'll show you when you go back to sleep."

I handed the now empty glass back to Lucien and he set it on a table next to the bed. Akira placed his hand on my back and I leaned into him. I yawned into my hand as I watched Lucien get into the bed and lean back against the headboard, he was still a few feet away from me.

"So, what's the plan? If this guy really is after me, we could set a trap."

"We could but I would rather not risk your life more than what we are already dealing with." He pulled a laptop off of the night table and opened it. "I've been reviewing the case and I think at this point, we need to try to find the crystal. If we can find it, we find our demon." He started opening some programs on his computer. "Akira and I went through my supplies and we have what we need to help build your circle."

"I thought you guys would have butted heads. That's what it looked like when I went up to the office with Uncle Ray. Don't take this the wrong way, I'm glad you're getting along." They seemed to be getting along, dare I say, they liked each other now?

"About that," Akira nudged my shoulder, "we agreed that you were more important over some silly guy posturing. He kept you safe, at the risk of his life, he's good with me." Akira pulled me into his lap, my legs draped off his sides and my feet were near Lucien.

Lucien cleared his throat and slid off the bed. "I'm going to go grab a sandwich, I'll give you some privacy." He closed the bedroom door behind him as he walked out. I was saddened that he left but the sight of him in those jeans and his bubble butt helped ease that sadness considerably.

He was giving us space to talk, or other things, and my heart swelled at his kindness. I squeezed my hands together. "Akira," I rested my head on his chest so I could listen to his heart beat, "I was really scared. If Lucien hadn't been there, I think I would have been victim number seven."

"I hate that I wasn't there to protect you." Akira put a finger under my chin and gently moved my face to look up at him. "But, according to bubble butt detective, you saved him too. You are far braver than you give yourself credit for. Not everyone would go back to help an injured person when escaping and you did. I am so proud of you." He kissed me so gently it brought tears to my eyes again.

I placed my hands on his chest. "Why do you always know what to say?"

"I'm amazing, obviously." His tone was deadpanned and he kept a straight face as he spoke.

"Akira!" Laughing I kissed his cheeks. "I love you so much. Also, bubble butt detective? How'd you come up with that?" It was eerily close to what I had been calling him in my head.

"Don't tell me you didn't notice he has a glorious bubble butt that just begs to be bitten."

If I had been drinking some water, I would have spit it out and choked on my laughter. I knew Akira was into men too but hadn't really thought about that until now. He wiggled his eyebrows together and pulled me closer, nuzzling my neck.

"Of course I noticed but I'm surprised you did."

"He's an exotic specimen of the male form. I'm not blind." His lips moved along my neck toward my shoulder. "I bet he tastes almost as good as you do." He sucked on my collarbone, dragging a gasp from me.

"Akira," I tugged on his hair, "wait. You've thought about kissing him?"

His deep chuckle sent heat straight between my legs. "Like you haven't?" He bit down where he had been sucking and started to unbutton my shirt. "You don't think about how it would feel to have him touch you like this?" He pulled my bra down, my breasts already aching even before he cupped them, rolling my nipples roughly between his fingers.

I dragged my nails down his side, already panting like I was in heat. I was clay in his hands, waiting for him to sculpt me. "Yes," I whisper, "I've thought about it."

Akira flicked my nipples with his thumbs. "Did you think about him sucking your nipples?" He leaned down taking my left nipple into his mouth, his tongue flicking it now instead of his thumb and I squirmed in his lap. His finger pinched my right nipple gently and pulled, I almost screamed.

"What did you think about detective bubble butt doing to you?" His mouth leaves my left nipple, drawing out a cry from me before moving to the right nipple. I was becoming so wet it was becoming uncomfortable and I ached for Akira.

"Please, Akira," I whimpered as he continued to torment me, "I need you inside of me." I pulled at his hair.

Akira continued to move between my nipples but he did move me so that I was lying beneath him. He held himself over me and pulled away blowing gently on my nipples teasingly. "You want the detective to do this to you?" His eyes were glazed and I couldn't hold back my shudder. "Tell me." He pulled my pants and panties down to my knees.

"Yes!" My hips bucked upward as his fingers pushed inside of me, stroking my pussy roughly. "I've thought of him fucking me!" Akira twisted his fingers inside of me dragging more cries from me. These thoughts had gone through my mind several times since meeting Lucien and I wanted it to be real. I was soon withering underneath him as he continued to pleasure me. His tongue flicked at my clit as he fucked my pussy with his fingers and it wasn't long before I shouted out his name as I came, my legs feeling like rubber.

Akira kissed me gently as he laid next to me, holding me close. "You're beautiful." He grinned down at me. "I hope these walls are thin and the detective heard you." His voice had deepened, his Texan accent making my pussy shudder again.

I blushed and sputtered. "What? Why? That's embarrassing."

"You didn't scream my name at the end. I hope he heard you." His grin turned wicked as I sat up.

"No, I cried out your name." I looked at him in horror as he shook his head. "I screamed Lucien's name out loud?" Now my voice was squeaking. It wasn't possible. Why was Akira ok with that? He had been pretty turned on by the thought of Lucien and me.

"You did," he was entirely too happy about it, "it was hot." He put his hands behind his head and laid back.

I rolled out of the huge bed and pulled my panties back up. "You, my love, are an asshole." I walked into the bathroom and closed the door.

"You loved it and I think we should talk about him." Akira's voice was confident and I could tell he was smirking.

I flushed the toilet and cleaned up the best I could. I looked in the mirror and had to blink for a second. My face was flushed, my hair was messy, and I looked happy. That angry puffball did this and he seemed like he might like Lucien too. That made me grin even more, I wondered if it would be as hot as I was thinking if they were to make out.

I went back into the bedroom and Akira was spread out on the bed horizontally. His eyes were closed and he looked peaceful. He had been running himself ragged with these patrols. I grabbed my pants, pulled them on, kissed his cheek gently, and went to find Lucien.

CHAPTER 8

*A*s I closed the bedroom door behind me, I glanced around.
Lucien's home was a ranch style house that was common in
Arizona. The floors were a beautiful grey wood but as I walked on
them barefoot, I discovered they were tile and cool to the touch. The
hallway led to a large living room that blended into an open kitchen.
Lucien was sitting on a large red couch that curled into an L with his
feet up, his laptop open, and his hair was out of its braid. It was the
first time I had seen his hair down and I wanted to run my fingers
through it. I wondered if he had heard us.

He looked up from the laptop and smiled but I could see how
tired he was. "Hey, you should be sleeping."

He shut the laptop and set it to the side and I noticed he had his
shirt unbuttoned. His chest was pretty much perfection. If Akira was
a yumsicle, Lucien was a pint of cremegasim. His chest was sculpted
and well defined, like the rest of him, and I could see his Adonis' belt
leading into his pants. My mouth went dry.

"Victoria?"

I shook my head side to side. "Sorry. I guess I'm just tired." I walked over to the couch and sat next to him, not quite touching but close enough to. "You know, you can call me Vickie, or V."

He shifted so he was facing me, giving a better view of his chest. "Thank you, Vickie." I swear his voice almost purred my name. "What are you doing up? Can't sleep?"

"I wanted to check on you. I feel bad that I kicked you out of your bed. Why are YOU still up? Do you ever sleep?"

Lucien shrugged, rubbing the back of his neck. "Sometimes but I don't sleep well when I have a case like this. But you don't need to bother yourself worrying about me."

I was touching his knee without thought and that electricity went right up my arm to my breasts making my nipples harder than they already were. "You won't help anyone if you fall over exhausted. Why don't I make some tea? You can relax and we can talk." I paused. "And not about the case, I'd like to get to know you more."

He stared down at my hand on his knee and was silent so long that I was about to get up when he placed his hand over mine. "I think I would like that but I'll make the tea. You're my guest." He stood after kissing my hand and went into the kitchen. I watched as his chestnut hair moved freely down his back. "Does chamomile work?"

"Sure, with a little honey?" He placed a tea kettle on the stove. "How old are you, Lucien?"

He pulled down a bag of tea and honey from a cupboard. "I guess we never discussed that, did we? I'm thirty three. I'm a native Arizonian and the only one in my family who still lives here."

"Tell me about your family?" He had seemed so sad when he talked about his sister before. "You said your mom was in your life and that was not common with wizard families?"

His movements flowed easily as he pulled the kettle from the stove as it started to whistle. "Yes, usually women are paid to carry children to term and after we are born, they leave. Wizards have strange traditions. But that wasn't the case with my mother." He came back into the living room carrying two mugs and handed one to me. "Careful, it's hot." He sat next to me and our legs touched. "My father fell in love during her pregnancy. He married her, against tradition. They had my sister three years later the traditional way. My sister isn't a wizard but is a powerful witch."

I blew the steam gently from my tea, taking a small sip. "What's your sister and nephews name?"

"Kaitlin and Alex." He smiled as his eyes looked off into a memory. "Alex is twelve now, I haven't seen him for four years now. She moved across the country to Georgia with her now ex-husband. He didn't like me because I always called him out on his bullshit so he forbade her to contact me. When they divorced, I thought maybe we could go back to the way we were before but she never replied to my mail, texts, or voicemails."

Anguish flew across his face and I took his hand in mine after placing my mug on the coffee table. "My parents said she'd come around but, as of now, she hasn't talked to any of us." He squeezed my hand and offered a heartbreakingly sad smile. I wanted to hug him and, possibly, punch his sister in the throat for causing him this pain. "Sorry, it's not exciting and just family drama."

I snorted. "You're kidding right? She's family. You obviously love her and Alex, it's painful for you to even talk about them. You know what my family dynamic is, so don't try to play it off. It's ok to hurt, it's ok to be mad and when you're ready to try again with her, I'll be here, cheering you on." I hugged his arm to my chest. "It's ok to have feelings, even if you're a big bad wizard detective."

Shock, followed quickly with a real smile passed across his face this time. "You're pretty amazing. You know that? I haven't talked about my sister and nephew to anyone except my parents, yet I tell you as if I've known you for years." He pulled his hand away from my arm hug and he caressed my cheek, the electric feel dancing between his fingers and my cheek.

"You just needed someone to listen." I closed my eyes, enjoying the touch of his hand when that electric feeling faded from my cheek, before I could open my eyes, lips pressed to mine for several seconds and the electric feeling from our lips passed through my body, making me shudder. I had to clench my legs together to stop from coming. He kissed me! He pulled back after a few seconds and I opened my eyes to find his face was right in front of mine.

His warm brown eyes with that golden rim searched mine and another smile, with dimples this time, was my undoing. I was in love with Lucien, as sure as I was in love with Akira.

"Thank you, Vickie." His voice was almost a whisper. "I think we should sleep. We have quite a few things to do tomorrow." He pressed his lips to mine again and I barely had to time to kiss him back before he was standing, taking our mugs to the kitchen sink. "I'll be sleeping on the couch. You and Akira can have the bed." He started to turn off the lights but waited at the hallway.

I stood on shaky legs and walked toward the bedroom but I stopped when I stood in front of him. I tipped my face up to meet his eyes again.

"This isn't over, you know that."

A playful smirk was my answer along with, "Oh, promises that I look forward to making sure come true." He waited until I went into his bedroom before he turned off the hallway light.

I crawled over Akira as I got into the bed after removing my bra and pants. He grunted as if I had jumped on him and I nudged my elbow into his stomach in retaliation. A soft laugh was his response and he pulled me close, my left leg going between his.

"It sounded like it went well with bubble butt." Akira murmured softly, his eyes still closed. "He even knows how to shut you up, so if I hadn't approved before, I would now."

I laughed and hit him with my pillow before settling down again.

"You're ok with me being in love with him?"

Akira opened his eyes and they almost glowed in the dark. "Of course. He makes you happy. I love you and I know you love me. You loving another doesn't diminish that. And you know that I like his body, I look forward to exploring it thoroughly while you watch."

"That's," I tried to think of something witty to say something back but I couldn't think of anything, "hot." I sighed.

His lips turned up, teeth flashing. "I know."

"Both of you are so cocky, you'll get along swimmingly." I smacked the arm that was under my pillow playfully. "Are you sure that it's ok and you're not just ok with this for me?"

Akira pulled my hair, pulling my face up and he kissed me roughly, biting my lower lip possessively. "What did I say? If I wasn't fine with it, you wouldn't be anywhere near him." And with that he pushed me on my other side and we spooned like the lovesick dorks we are.

"Goodnight." I whispered as I fell asleep with thoughts of both of the men in the house.

*I*t was shortly after noon when I woke up, took a quick shower, and dressed in the clothes Akira had packed for me. I could still feel my eye twitching with annoyance at him. He had packed all the graphic tees that I had since high school that were too tight and my breasts threatened to rip the fabric. But it was either the clean tees or my shirt from yesterday that was stinky and gross. I had pulled on the loosest shirt, which wasn't by much, that had Donatello from The Teenage Mutant Ninja Turtles on it.

Akira was in the living room, reading the book that he had brought with him. He was lounging on the couch, his limbs loose, but it was his clothing that had me blinking for a few seconds. He was wearing jeans that looked like they were painted on him and a muscle tank that showed off his perfect biceps and clung to his stomach, highlighting his abs. They were tight and possibly too small.

He flashed me a grin at me before returning to his book. Lucien was in the kitchen, it looked like he was putting together a quick brunch of cereal and fruit. It wasn't until I saw Lucien looking at Akira out of the corner of his eye when he didn't think he was watching when it hit me why Akira was dressed like a slut for hire. He was trying to seduce Lucien with his body. I had to turn around and quickly bite my hand to stop the laughter that threatened to overflow. My angry puffball was pulling out all the stops to get into Lucien's pants.

"Good morning." I turned around after composing myself and sat a little away from Akira so that Lucien would have to sit between us. He didn't have a dining table or barstool, so it looked like he used the coffee table when he ate.

"Good morning sunshine, the earth says hello." Akira didn't look up from his book.

I snorted. "Really? Charlie and the Chocolate Factory?" He was such a dork.

"Mmm. It seemed appropriate." He placed his book on the coffee table as Lucien came into the room, balancing four bowls between his hands. Akira stood and grabbed two of the bowls and flashed his teeth at Lucien. "Thanks for feeding us."

"It's the least I can do." Lucien acted like he hadn't been eyeing Akira in the kitchen. He placed a bowl of Lucky Charms in front of me and the other bowl held the fruit, which he laid on the table between all of us. He thanked Akira when he gave Lucien his bowl of cereal and I watched in amusement as Akira made sure to touch Lucien's fingers.

"I love Lucky Charms." I grinned at Lucien as he sat next to me. I noticed he was closer to me than Akira. "I usually steal Akira's marshmallows."

Akira huffed and started to eat his cereal. "You're not getting these marshmallows and Lola isn't here to help you take them."

"Lola?" Lucien's amusement was evident as he looked between us. "Who is that?" He picked up his spoon and picked out a few of the marshmallows and put them into my bowl.

I blushed looking at him, feeling warm. "Thank you. See, Akira. Lucien is willing to give me his marshmallows." I stick my tongue out at him. "Lola is my best friend. She's a pixie." I finished my cereal quickly, I was hungry.

"Maybe I want his marshmallows too." Akira replied dryly but Lucien choked on the spoonful he had just swallowed at Akira's horrible sexual innuendo.

"Oh my god," Lucien laughed as I smacked his back a few times to help clear his airway, "that was horrible!" His laugh was contagious and we all were laughing soon. It was several minutes later before the laughter subsided but Akira was still snickering.

"It was horrible, wasn't it?" He puffed his chest out, proud of the pick-up line that had made Lucien choke and us all to laugh.

I was shaking my head when there was suddenly a loud thunder-clap outside and I jumped. When I looked out to the backyard, the sun was shining and there were hardly any clouds. "Did you guys hear that?"

"Hear what, love?" Akira placed his finished bowl on the coffee table.

"The thunder." Another loud clap of thunder echoed and this time I felt the room shake. "You can't hear that?" I had to hold my hands over my ears as another boomed out.

"It's a vision fighting to show itself to you." Siobal was suddenly in front of me. "You need more magical energy to have it manifest, otherwise it's going to continue as it is now."

I had forgotten that I had gotten some type of power from Siobal.

I whimpered. "Siobal is here. She says it's a vision but I need more magical energy before it will work." The next clap of thunder went on for several seconds.

Lucien was on his feet and he pushed the coffee table with our bowls against the far wall. "Akira, can you move the couch against the backdoor?" He was already striding out of the room toward another room in the back. He appeared seconds later with a large piece of chalk.

Akira gently moved me to the side of the room where the coffee table had been pushed and he easily shoved the large couch against the opposite wall where the backdoor was. Lucien got on his hands and knees and started to draw an intricate circle on the floor.

The circle was only four feet in diameter but he inlaid spell wards inside of the circle. As he worked, the thunder seemed to get louder and it felt like the ground shook. Akira came over to my side and placed his arm around my waist, offering comfort and it helped to ground my focus. It only took Lucien a few minutes to finish all but the last line of the circle but it felt like an eternity as the thunder kept going off around me.

"Vickie, will you come over? Step over the circle but make sure not to smudge any of the line work." He offered up his free hand from where he still kneeled on the floor. I took it and carefully stepped into the circle. "Now, if you can sit and cross your legs like you did the first night when you tried meditating with me for the first time." He squeezed my hand before letting it go and he finished the last line of the circle, sealing it. "Now, clear your mind. Focus only on your breathing. In and out. Ignore everything else."

I close my eyes and start to breathe in and out slowly. The noise from the thunder claps slowly faded as I tried to block everything out. It wasn't as easy to empty my mind as Lucien said but I had to. To make the noise go away and for Siobal and the other victims.

Soon all I felt and knew was breathing deep and slow. There was a buzzing under my skin, it felt like the thunder claps that had been outside were now inside of me. Breath in. Buzzing clap. Breath out. Clap. I don't know how long this went on, the buzzing in my skin was not unpleasant but it got stronger and stronger.

"Vickie," Siobal's voice was soft, bringing me back from wherever I was. "You're literally glowing again with magic."

I lifted my hands and tilted my head in awe as my eyes opened. She was right, I was glowing. I knew I should be concerned, or even excited, about this but all I felt was calm and enjoyed the buzzing within my body.

"Vickie, what are you feeling?"

"There's a buzzing in me, under my skin. I feel calm, nothing is bothering me anymore."

Siobal was floating in front of me, sitting like I was. She looked at me with an expression of pride. "That's a vision, you're ready. Think about what you want to know and sink into it."

I nodded. I wanted to know where the killer was and how we could stop him. That's all that mattered. We had to stop him from hurting anyone else.

The buzzing under my skin sharpened and suddenly I wasn't in Lucien's living room and the buzzing cut off. There was a voice speaking but I couldn't make out the words, it was like I was underwater, but the voice was familiar. It almost sounded like my ex-boyfriend, Shax. Why was he in this vision? But just like that, his voice disappeared.

I glanced around noticing that wherever I was had tall ceilings, metal walls, concrete floors, and was empty except for a small area in the middle where what looked like bags of trash, an old chair, papers, and a strange looking staff like object was strewn across the floor. I couldn't see any color, just black, grey, and white. I walked toward the middle of the room when there was a loud screeching noise of a large door opening.

Looking toward the noise, a large door was being opened to the right. It was one of those industrial metal doors that are almost as high as the ceiling and had to slide to open.

I was in a warehouse, that explained the metal door and high ceilings. A tall figure in a cloak strolled in toward the items in the center of the room. It was just dark enough that I wasn't able to see a face underneath the hood but I did see the hands that were long claws. It was him, our killer and demon. There was no one else around so the one who summoned him must not be around. I felt that was significant but I couldn't remember why while in this vision.

The demon sprawled in the old chair, kicking papers away. I moved closer to see if I could look under the hood. The demon made a loud grunt and pulled out a Ziplock bag from a pocket. What was in that bag would cause me to throw up after I was out of this vision. The bag was filled with eyeballs and the demon opened it and took one out, throwing it into his mouth. I saw a glimpse of sharpened teeth. There was a squish sound as the demon ate. I was in front of him now but still couldn't see anything under the hood except for the teeth that should have belonged in a piranha's mouth.

My foot touched the staff object that was next to the chair. Now that I was closer, it was a curious looking thing. It was long, probably five feet and the top part of it curled before sharpening off to a point. There were grooves carved along the staff and a place to hold it was in the middle, worn from use. The most curious thing about this staff though was that it was made of some type of stone, not wood. Everything was grey around me but as I focused on the staff, color started to almost bleed through. I leaned closer, it looked like it was made of an impossibly large ruby, but that couldn't be right, could it?

The demon made a grunting noise and as I looked back at it, it had its hands under its robes stroking itself. That was not what I wanted to see but just as quickly as it started the demon finished and stood again. Talk about a short fuse.

I stepped back as it stood and that's when I saw a crystal, about the length of my index finger, draped on a chain around its neck. That had to be Siobal's.

It grabbed the staff and walked to the door to leave. The buzzing in my skin was back and I closed my eyes instinctively knowing that the vision was about to end. The buzzing increased sharply and suddenly cut off.

I opened my eyes and was back in Lucien's home with Siobal, Akira, and Lucien in front of me, just outside of the circle. "Hi guys." My throat felt parched. "That was a trip." And I threw up as I remembered the eyeballs.

"*I*'m so sorry, Lucien." The living room was back to normal after a quick cleaning spell and I was laying on the couch with my head in Akira's lap with a cool rag on my forehead while Akira stroked my hair. "That was gross." I held my hand in front of my face as I looked at my skin. It was still glowing but Akira said it was fading, apparently while I had been in the middle of the vision, I was almost blinding.

"You didn't do anything wrong." Akira leaned forward to kiss my cheeks gently. "Just relax."

Lucien had my feet in his lap. "I agree with Akira. There's nothing to be sorry for. I'm just glad you're feeling better." As he stroked my legs, offering comfort, it did the exact opposite and was turning me on. I kept my eyes closed, trying to focus.

"And if what you saw was true, we have a solid lead on finding this demon. I've sent the report to headquarters and they are doing some research on that staff you described." His hands moved from my legs to my bare feet and I lost all sense for several seconds as he started to massage them. I couldn't hold back a moan and he just chuckled softly, pressing his thumbs into the bottom of my feet.

"Oh, that's heaven." I felt like a puddle. He had turned me into a gooey puddle with just his hands. I could only imagine what his tongue could do. "I'll be your maid for the rest of your life if you promise not to stop rubbing my feet." Another soft moan escaped my lips, almost a sigh.

"Don't stop," Akira rumbled above my head, "I want to see her in a French maid outfit so bad." His fingers pressed gently on my temples, rubbing in a circular motion. "That's every guys dream, right, detective?"

I opened my eyes to squint up at him suspiciously. What was he up to? He just gave me a smug smile.

"It's a tempting offer," Lucien voice was velvet, "I'll think about it." His tone was serious and I swallowed quietly. "But, back to the topic at hand," I felt Akira huff, "not seeing the summoner near the demon is concerning. When a demon is summoned, they are bound to the person as their master and that means the demon can never be too far from their master. It's a myth that demons are given orders and can go about it on their own. There's not been a free demon on Earth in centuries where the demon had free reign. The link between the two would make sure of that and if the demon tried, the link would cause extreme pain to their essence." That was only slightly frightening to think about.

"And what about hearing her ex-boyfriends voice?" Akira really didn't like Shax.

"If you only heard a voice," Siobal spoke up, "it may mean you need to contact him. The vision wouldn't show you something that's not important to your question."

"I was afraid of that," I sighed and gently pulled my feet from Lucien's lap and sat up, "I need to call him. His voice wouldn't have been in my vision if he wasn't important to this."

"I am assuming there's history with Shax that you would rather keep in the past?" Lucien tilted his head just enough that some hair that was loose from his braid fell into his face as he pulled open his laptop.

"That's an understatement." Akira grumbled and he stared out the window.

I placed a hand on his thigh and squeezed in comfort. "I'm over it, Akira. It was years ago and I don't have to worry about him anymore. I have the two of you now."

Lucien's head whipped up from the laptop as Akira glanced back over to me and started to laugh. Damn my mouth and its inability to filter!

"I mean that I'm working with the two of you now so it's not a big deal." I tried to play it off confidently but I'm pretty sure they both could see through it.

Lucien cleared his throat. "I see." A grin tugged at his lips and he looked back down at his laptop.

Akira, on the other hand, was still laughing, the asshat. He always enjoyed when I would say something awkward and would tease me mercilessly about it later and this would be no different, I was sure. I swatted at his thigh as I stood up.

"I might as well do it now. I'm going to grab my phone in the room. I'll be right back." I might have put a little stalk into my step as I left the room to Akira's snickering.

My cell phone was charging on the night stand near the bathroom. As I unplugged it, I checked my text messages and saw that I had missed a few from Lola and Uncle Ray. I took a few minutes to reply to each. Lola was feeling better and had heard about the bar closing, she had wanted to know if I was going to be ok for rent next month. She may be doom and gloom to other people but she was a beautiful soul. Uncle Ray wanted to know how I was feeling and told me to tell Akira not to slack off. After the replies were sent, I pulled up my contact list and scrolled through until I pulled up Shax's contact labeled, "Demon Spawn Shit Face" and pressed the call button before I chickened out.

CHAPTER 9

*I*t only rang three times before he picked up and at the sound of his familiar voice brought up nostalgic memories of picnics under the stars in the desert, midnight movies in the last drive thru movie theater in the Valley, and passionate but unskilled love making in Hot Topic dressing rooms in high school.

"Vic?" His voice had deepened from the last time we had spoken. "This is a surprise. Are you alright?"

The saliva in my mouth had dried up, my tongue felt heavy and it took several tries to answer him. "Shax, I'm ok." I wasn't sure how to go about this, I probably should have thought it out more before dialing him.

There was silence on both of our ends. "Vic, as nice as it is to hear your voice, I know you didn't call me because you missed me." I imagined the longing I thought I heard in his tone. "What's up?"

I took a calming breath. "I need your help. Some things have happened." I proceeded to go over the full story with him, not leaving anything out. It took a little over ten minutes to get the whole story out and the whole time he didn't interrupt, just listened quietly. "So, that's what happened. I heard your voice in my vision."

"I knew about the killings; it's been all over the Supe's news but I didn't think you'd find a way to get involved." There was the dry tact I remembered. "It shouldn't be a surprise, though." I couldn't tell if he was being sarcastic or serious. "I'm in Nevada, at the moment, but I'll leave first thing tomorrow morning. It'll take about six or seven hours to get there. I'll help you, Vic, but not for free."

"What do you want? I can talk to Lucien to see if the MEPA will pay you." If there was one thing about Shax that hadn't changed, he was always looking for a deal.

"Not money. Time. With you. We have things to go over from the past and this time, you're not running away to hide behind the pack." I could hear the determination in his voice and I winced inwardly.

The last thing I wanted to do was talk about the past with him but if that's what it took to get his help, whatever my vision required from him, I would bite the bullet and do it. Maybe keep Akira away though, that way there would be no punching and intestines pulled out.

"Fine, deal."

"Great. I'll see you tomorrow afternoon at the bar." I heard a click and he had ended the conversation just like that.

Well. That was that. My ex-boyfriend was going to help us catch a demon that eats its victims' eyeballs as snacks. This was like a horror episode of Scooby Doo without the awesome Great Dane.

I pulled my hair out of its ponytail and braided it as I thought about Shax. We had met when I was seventeen when he had transferred into our school. It would have been hard on anyone transferring into a new school in their senior year but Shax was enigmatic and everyone loved him. Even being a quarter demon, he was one of the stronger magic users in school, so all the girls labeled him as a bad boy. The other boys either hated him or wanted to be his best friend.

The first time I had run into him was in the middle of math class when I was asked to get some textbooks from another teacher across the campus. I hate math, so it was an easy way to get out of class. I had been walking back when I had tripped over a nonexistent rock,

(I'm not admitting that it was just me being clumsy) and Shax had been passing by me and caught me before I nose-dived into the concrete. He even managed to catch a few of the books before they fell to the ground.

For me, it was love at first sight, even though I was crushing on Akira. Shax told me later that he had felt the same way and he knew my feelings for Akira were always there and had always said as long as I was with him and not Akira, he didn't care.

We became inseparable within days, walking to class together, going to social events, dates every night. We dated through the rest of high school and when we graduated, he went to college and I started working for Uncle Ray. When my plans for NAU fell through, he had transferred to ASU so that he would still be close.

Unlike when Akira and Lucien touch me, when Shax touched me it felt like fire dancing under my skin. Contrary to a lot of people's gossip, we didn't start having sex until we graduated high school. Shax had driven us up to Flagstaff and had rented a cabin for the weekend right before Christmas. It had been beautiful, sweet, and unforgettable.

Fast forward a few years and it was right before my twenty second birthday. I was certain he was finally going to ask me to marry him. Shax had made plans for us to go to dinner before my party at the bar. I had worn a dress I had saved for three months to buy for this occasion but I had known he would love it. I arrived at his place early and let myself in. He had been in his room on the phone. I hadn't wanted to interrupt so I was quiet and sat on the couch but I could still hear his conversation.

"Dad, I know. I'm almost done with school. I'll come home. Victoria? No. You don't need to worry about her. She's just been a play thing for me, you know how I get bored and it was easier to string one girl along rather than waste time worrying about other women."

I thought I was dying from pain as my heart cracked in two. I had run out of the apartment and when I wouldn't answer his phone calls when the time had passed for our dinner reservation, he showed up at the bar. I was crying in Uncle Ray's arms and Akira had met him at the door with a fist to his face, breaking his nose. Akira had let him know to never contact me again or he'd rip him limb from limb. It hadn't been a threat but a promise. He'd still tried to call me and text me for weeks after but I would just delete the texts and voicemails without listening to them.

And here we were, four years later, he was coming to the bar to help me because I had asked him to. It was time to go back and tell the guys that Shax had agreed to help and would be here tomorrow afternoon. I finished braiding my hair as I walked back into the living room.

Lucien was straddling Akira who still sat on the couch, and had his hands pulling his shirt forward and his mouth was fastened over Akira's. My mouth dropped in shock as I watched Lucien deepen the kiss, I could see their tongues fighting each other. He tipped Akira's face back as he straddled him and Akira's hands wrapped around his back and down to cup his ass, squeezing tightly.

I had obviously missed how this started but I was not going to complain. Lucien's hands moved from Akira's shirt to around his neck. Akira growled low in pleasure and his hands, still on Lucien's ass, pulled him tighter against him. Soon Lucien's hips moved in thrusting motions and they were dry humping each other as the kiss they shared started to become sloppy, I could hear them start breathing harder. My right hand slid inside my pants under my panties. I was already wet watching them making out.

Akira pulled away from the kiss, making Lucien almost hiss in frustration but it turned into a moan as Akira moved his lips to his neck, licking and nipping at his skin. They were still moving together in a rushed rocking motion. Lucien arched his back suddenly as Akira bit down on his lower neck, marking him with this teeth. I started rubbing my clit as I watched Akira move his hands to the front of Lucien's jeans and I heard the zipper being pulled down. I didn't move closer to see because I didn't want them to see me and stop.

"Gods, you're so hard." Akira practically purred up at him, making Lucien moan. Akira's arm was moving so he must have been stroking Lucien's cock. I was soon pressing my fingers against my clit in rough circular movements, matching Akira's movements. Lucien's hands moved to grasp Akira's biceps, his nails digging into them. The only sound in the room was our heavy breathing.

"Come for me, detective." Akira's voice cracked out in his authoritative voice and Lucien's face grimaced in pleasure and within several seconds his body jerked as he cried out Akira's name. I came at the sound of Lucien's pleasure, shuddering violently where I stood.

Akira's voice was happy. "Mmm. You're even prettier when you come." His hand that had brought Lucien pleasure moved to his mouth and he licked his fingers clean as Lucien and I watched.

"That went farther than I meant to." Lucien sounded winded. "Not that I'm complaining." He sat back on Akira's legs.

"That was so hot." I had pulled my hand out of my pants and walked over to them. Lucien practically jumped off of Akira's lap but was pulled back by Akira.

"You watched?" Lucien zipped his pants up and he offered an almost shy smile to me.

"Sorry?" Not really.

Akira pulled Lucien forward into his lap more and stroked his hands down his back. "You enjoyed the show. I can smell it." He smirked evilly as I blushed.

"Yes, I did. What happened when I was in the bedroom on the phone?"

"I decided not to beat around the bush and just tell our detective bubble butt that we wanted him. He didn't know if he felt the same." He turned his smirk toward Lucien. "We both knew that was just him posturing. So, I dared him if he could kiss me and not feel a thing, we wouldn't bother him about it again. Oh, and fifty dollars." Then he did something tender and sweet. He pulled Lucien down and kissed him gently for a few seconds. "You owe me fifty bucks."

"Detective bubble butt?" Lucien pulled back, "bubble butt?" I couldn't tell if he was offended by the nickname or found it entertaining.

"You have a glorious ass. Why not let us call you by it?" There was Akira, ever the man of words and honesty.

Lucien's shoulders started to jerk and I thought that he was having some kind of medical attack but a chortle slid out from his mouth before he was laughing loudly that his head was thrown back. "Detective Bubble Butt. Oh my gods, if my father heard that he would have a heart attack." He gasped out in between his laughter. Akira sat there, still smirking and holding Lucien by his hips.

I sat on the couch next to them and waited while Lucien finished laughing. It was nice to see him laugh so much this past day. I had a feeling since we met, he didn't get to enjoy himself very often in his line of work. Learning about his estranged family and how sad it made him just made me want to hug him and see him smile and laugh more. Akira caught my eye and winked. He was a cocky asshat but he was mine, and now, if Lucien would agree, his too.

Lucien sobered after several minutes and he stood from Akira's lap and sat on the coffee table, facing us. His arms rested on his knees and he laced his fingers together. The joyful feeling had left and was replaced with a seriousness that pierced straight through me as he met my eyes before looking at Akira.

"I can't make any promises. Not while working this case." I sucked in my breath ready to fight for him but he held up a hand before I could speak. "But," his lips quirked, "I know that I want to pursue this. I've never been with more than one person at a time, but I'm not opposed to being with you two."

My shoulders relaxed, the worry falling away and I felt Akira relax next to me.

"I am attracted to both of you. I know that the feelings I have for you, Vickie, are on such an unprofessional level that if my bosses could read my mind, I would be flayed alive and my magic stripped." His lips moved to a full on grin, his dimples showing. "And obviously,

I want Akira to put my money to good use." Akira flashed his teeth and when I glanced at his lap, he was still hard. Lucien took my hand in his left and took Akira's in his right. "I'm not usually into sharing, so if we are going to do this, I won't allow anyone else to touch either of you, you're mine and I'm yours."

I shivered. Commanding Lucien was hot. I nodded. "Same here. You don't get to go out, or have sex, with others, except us."

"As long as we all agree, can we go fuck each other's brains out now?" Akira thickened his Texan accent and spoke slow. "I'm about to burst."

This time I laughed along with Lucien. He stood and pulled on our hands to stand. I was quivering in anticipation already. Glancing between the two of them I couldn't believe my luck. They were both mine and all other women could suck it.

"I'm sure we have a few hours before I hear back from headquarters." Lucien's lowered his voice and pulled me toward him.

I was suddenly in his arms and his mouth was slanted across mine, his tongue dominating mine. He tasted fresh, like spring, and I pressed my breasts into his chest, my nipples aching they were so hard. I knew he felt them through the thin shirt I wore and he moaned. My head swam, I couldn't focus on anything except his mouth on mine, his tongue stroking inside, sending that thrilling electricity throughout my body.

Lucien suddenly picked me up, my legs wrapping around his waist instinctively. His mouth moved from my mouth to my jawline and up to my ear. His tongue licked along my ear and his voice sent hot breath onto my ear and I almost came with the feeling as I cried out.

"Let's go to the bedroom." He walked to his room. "You too, Akira." He looked back, hunger in his gaze. "I want you to take her with me."

"You don't need to tell me twice." Akira's rough voice was right behind us as we went into the bedroom.

Lucien set me down gently and before I could move, he and

Akira were removing my clothing. Lucien pulled my shirt off and he unhooked my bra with one hand, color me impressed. Akira tugged my pants and panties off, none too gently but I didn't care. I just wanted them inside of me. Akira kissed me, almost feverishly, and I was suddenly airborne, he had tossed me onto the bed. I opened my mouth to give him a piece of my mind but Lucien was in front of me, naked, and all thought fled my mind.

He had a scant peppering of light brown hair across his chest, his nipples were dark and hard, and his Adonis's belt was the perfect V shape. I was touching his chest and moving my fingers down the natural V toward his cock before I could think. I just wanted to touch him. And to taste him. His cock was hard and circumcised. I briefly wondered if wizard magic did that or if he'd had surgery and I giggled.

"Does my cock really amuse you that much?" Lucien raised an eyebrow at me.

"No, I just," but I didn't get to say anything else because Akira was next to Lucien and seeing both of them in all their glory would bring any sex crazed woman to her knees. "Oh."

"I think she's just overwhelmed by it." Akira's eyes flashed teasingly. "I think you should touch him, V. Let him feel your touch, it's only fair considering I had first dibs."

My hand closed around Lucien's cock and we both shuddered. He wasn't as thick as Akira but his cock was perfection. I rubbed his tip, pressing my fingertips lightly against his slit at the top and his breath hitched. I watched as Akira kissed Lucien as I stroked his cock, their tongues were visible and I felt Lucien's cock twitching. I pushed Akira gently away with my other hand and pulled Lucien on top of me, stroking him faster.

"Nah uh, Akira. You got to make him come already. It's my turn." I kissed along his chest as I brought both hands down to his cock.

Lucien huffed out a laugh that morphed into a groan. "You're both going to be the death of me." He pulled away from my hands, kissing me hard. "Do you need a condom, Akira?"

Akira was laying on his side, stroking my sides. "Mm. No. Shifters don't carry diseases and Vic had a contraceptive spell cast on her when she first started having sex."

And I had. My mother and I may not get along, but she at least taught me to be responsible with my body. She had cast a spell that prevented pregnancy until I dispelled it.

"Ok, no condoms." Lucien was still over me and trailed kisses along my neck. "Good to know." He rolled off to my other side and pulled me so that Akira was now presented my backside and I was facing Lucien. "Forgive me, but I don't think I can do much more foreplay. Akira, the nightstand has lube, if you'd like to get her ready for you."

"Ready for him?" I was moving my fingers along his chest, distracted and not paying attention to the conversation.

Akira's breath on the back of my neck made me shiver. "We're both going to be inside of you beautiful and I don't plan on hurting you." He pressed a finger against my ass and I realized what he meant and I got even hotter, my pussy already soaking. I had always enjoyed having sex with both entrances, now it was going to happen at once.

"Well, hurry it up, would you?" I demanded. I wanted to feel both of them.

Lucien claimed my lips again with his and his long fingers stroked my thighs, teasingly running on the outside of my pussy. My hips moved to follow his fingers, my legs opening for him. Akira's warm hand was on my ass cheek, kneading gently and I moaned as I felt him press a finger inside of me as Lucien's fingers thrust into my pussy.

It was a new feeling with both entrances being filled and my legs shook. Lucien pulled his mouth away moving to my chest and he continued to pull on my nipples using his teeth and tongue as his instruments. Lucien was gentle as he went from each nipple, only teasing me, which was torture. He was thrusting his fingers inside of me, matching Akira's as he pressed another finger into me from behind and there was only pleasure after the first few seconds of pain as he worked with Lucien. I felt Akira's lips moving up my neck from behind and I turned my head so that he could kiss me. I was so close to coming that I wanted to cry out.

"I think she's ready." Akira pulled back from our kiss and slid fingers from inside of me and I did cry out at the loss. He grinned down at me and I heard a cap being closed and he lay against my back again, he had poured more lube and was working it along his cock.

"Good, I'm about to burst." Lucien pulled his fingers from my pussy with a slick sound. I was about to demand they stop teasing again when they both were inside of me with one stroke. I hadn't been ready and I stopped breathing as I let out a whimper of pleasure. My hands clenched and my nails dug into Lucien's chest. I was so full that the feeling was overwhelming.

"Oh gods," Lucien's voice cracked, "how is she so tight?" His hips pulled back and thrust back inside of me. Akira was soon thrusting inside of me in opposite strokes and I lost my mind. I couldn't think, I couldn't move, I couldn't remember my own name as they used my body as their own.

Akira's hand curled under my leg and pulled it over his and he was inside of me deeper. I felt my orgasm building inside of me that it almost hurt. Lucien's hand was on my clit, rubbing in circles as his own strokes inside of me became more erratic and I could hear his breathing become more ragged.

Akira's thrusts became harder, his skin slapping against mine and I knew he was close to. I kissed Lucien frantically, sucking on his tongue as I felt my release build higher. I came and as soon as I did, their thrusts became synchronized and several moments later, as I was still in the throes of my release, they both found theirs.

"Shit." Akira happily exclaimed as he pulled out of me and he didn't even sound winded. "That was fantastic. Vic, you took us both like a champ."

I raised a fist in the air. "Hoorah." They both laughed and I enjoyed several deep kisses from both of them in response. "Next time, one of you is in the middle." I teased but was also completely serious.

"Sounds like a plan to me." Lucien took my cheeks in his hands and his forehead met mine. "This was amazing and you're more beautiful than I dreamed." This man was going to get ravaged when I had the strength again. "Let's go get cleaned up."

J was lounging against Akira's chest in the large bath tub. The water was hot and there were bubbles. I was certain I had died and gone to heaven.

"You certainly enjoy the larger things in life." Akira arms were spread along the edges of the tub and Lucien was leaning against his side. "This is larger than Akira's tub."

Lucien stifled a yawn. "I like the small pleasures. A jetted tub is just one of those." He laid his head on Akira's forearm. "When I'm home I don't have to worry about work or other things. Usually."

"Well, I approve." Akira kissed the top of my head.

I stretched my legs out and floated up. "Um, I called Shax. He's agreed to come help us however he can. He'll be here tomorrow afternoon." I floated away from Akira's chest and yelped when Lucien pulled me into his lap. "Hi, Bubble Butt." I looked up at him and laughed when he just shook his head.

"I'll be interested to see how your ex-boyfriend can help us catch this demon. Even if he is a quarter demon, I doubt he will have more information than MEPA." It sounded like Akira had talked a little about Shax with him. "The other information you saw will most likely help us catch this killer." Lucien leaned forward and kissed me, biting my lower lip. "Have I thanked you for helping me?"

"Hmm, I don't think so. I think Akira hasn't been thanked yet, either." I looked over at Akira.

"I'll have to correct that." Lucien proceeded to show his gratitude with his fingers and mouth.

CHAPTER 10

*T*he next morning I woke up first and went into the kitchen to make breakfast. I was sore and achy but it was the greatest feeling in the world. When I opened the fridge and saw the meager offerings, I decided that Lucien needed some groceries.

I dressed quietly, wrote a note, left it on the pillow between my two men, and headed out. They were both zonked out. Although I took a few minutes to enjoy the view of Lucien laying on his stomach with his arm stretched out toward the middle of the bed where I had been and Akira laying on his back, snoring.

Akira had driven his truck over so I borrowed it. I wasn't worried about the demon tracking me, he hadn't killed any of his victims during the day and when he had attacked us at Siobal's townhouse it had been sunset.

There was a local grocery store only a few miles away. One thing you learn when growing up in Arizona, it doesn't matter what time of day it is, the grocery stores are always packed. I ended up having to park Akira's truck pretty far back and with the heat and humidity I was soaked with sweat by the time I got inside.

I grabbed a cart and decided to start at the fruits and vegetables. I couldn't buy a full house of groceries; I was just a bartender. But I could buy a few days' worth of groceries and not worry about it breaking the bank. I wasn't the greatest cook but I could make a mean pork chop with Spanish rice. I tend to shop with my stomach if I'm hungry so I ended up tossing in Little Debbie snacks and some chips and a case of soda. Even with the extras it didn't end up too expensive.

I sent a text to Akira's phone, even though he was probably still sleeping, letting him know I was on my way back in a few minutes. It didn't take too long to check out, bag the groceries and head outside back into the sweltering heat. Even if you're in the best of shape, after walking for a bit in this heat and humidity you start to gasp a little bit. I was happy to get inside of the truck and turn the AC on full blast.

I was just about to put the car into reverse and get out of there when I saw a familiar, but annoying, figure. Carl the nasty tempered gnome, was strutting along the sidewalk like the heat didn't affect him. Gnomes used a glamour like the rest of the community when out in the world with humans but I couldn't tell if he had one cast or not. If the looks some of the humans passing him were any indication, he didn't have one up. I cursed low and put the truck into reverse backing out of the space and back into drive as quickly as I could. I pulled up along the sidewalk and rolled down the window.

"Carl!" I hissed out. "Your glamour isn't working!"

He looked up at the truck and he flashed his teeth. "Well, well. If it isn't my favorite bartender." He stopped walking and placed his hands on his hips. "I was so sad that the bar was closed last night."

His voice had a strange roughness to it than I had heard before. His teeth flashed again at me. "Sure hope that it opens soon!" He flicked a hand in the air and his glamour slid into place seamlessly. "See you soon, Victoria."

I prayed no humans had seen when he did. I huffed at him, not answering him about the bar and drove away, looking out at him from the rearview mirror. He was at least keeping his glamour up. I'd need to remember to tell Uncle Ray about it. Even though each race was monitored by their own people, Uncle Ray was usually the one to call for any issues in the Phoenix area.

By the time I pulled back into Lucien's driveway, I had been gone only about an hour. I took a moment to look at the outside of his house. It was a ranch style, but it had a bell roof and round tower as the entryway. The landscaping was overflowing with different colored flowers and looked like they had been just thrown in for splashes of color that worked. It made me smile, it was such a Lucien thing to do.

Lucien was in the kitchen when I opened the door with the groceries. He almost dropped his mug of tea as he rushed over to me.

"Vickie, why did you leave without one of us? We can't protect you if we aren't with you." He sounded frustrated bordering on anger. "That was reckless." He took the grocery bags from me and stormed back into the kitchen. "The demon could have found you. You could be his next target!" He was slamming cupboards as he put food away. "It would have taken us all of five minutes to pull some clothes on to go with you."

I had to pause as I closed the door behind me. I had been perfectly safe, or as safe as anyone could be in a crowded grocery store as long as you don't get between the coupon moms and the deals.

Akira walked in from the hallway, his jeans unbuttoned and falling down. His hair was standing up and I started to walk over to him but he wore a glare and it was directed at me. My angry puffball was really angry.

"Victoria," Yup, full name from Akira meant I was in trouble, "we got your note and I got your text, but please, tell me what was going through your head?" Akira's voice was calm but I could hear the unbridled cold rage lying just underneath. "I'm pretty sure when Ray ordered that you be protected, you were there."

I winced and walked into the living room and sat down. "I didn't think it would be such a big deal. There were people around and it is the middle of the morning. The demon hasn't attacked anyone during the day, when he went after us at Siobal's it was almost night time." I knew they were angry because they were worried but I could take care of myself. I looked back up and met his gaze. "I'm not an invalid, nor am I stupid. I am a grown woman who can make her own decisions. I let you know where I was going, which wasn't far. I left during the morning and during a heavy traffic period. The demon isn't going to try to kill me with so many humans around. I also sent you a text when I was done and, on the way back. I was trying to do something nice for Lucien. Have you seen his fridge?" I stood back up and stomped into the kitchen and gestured to the food that was in there now. "This is all from my trip. Were we supposed to eat cereal and order take out while we're here?"

"Vickie," Lucien took a deep breath and came up behind me, "I'm sorry I snapped at you. We woke up and you were gone. We saw your note and were about to call you when you sent us that text." He wrapped his arms around me from behind and he rested his chin on top of my head. "Just wake one of us up if you want to go somewhere next time?"

I sighed and leaned into his arms. "Next time, huh?" I placed my hands over his. "That sounds like you might be planning to stick around, Detective Lucien."

He pulled his right hand from under mine and tipped my chin back and over to look at him. "I plan on sticking around for a long time. We'll catch this demon, close the case, and I get to claim that I got the girl in the end." A loud snort came from the other side of the bar and Lucien smiled. "And I got the guy, too." He pressed our lips together and with a slip of tongue later my knees felt woozy, I wasn't annoyed anymore and I could grudgingly agree I should have woken them, not that I was going to tell them that.

"Now, if we're done agreeing that Vickie will go with us wherever she goes until this guy is caught," Akira entered the kitchen, "why don't I make some breakfast? I saw you got everything I need to make Texas French Toast, hmm?" He pulls me from Lucien and kissed me hard, biting my lower lip, like he would nip an adolescent shifter. "I don't want to think about losing you. Alright?"

I nodded. "I'm sorry I upset you."

"Alright," Lucien yawned. "Now that we have that all done, I'm going to strengthen the wards around the house and breakfast sounds fantastic." He went to walk out of the kitchen but Akira tugged on his braid and pulled him back. "Hey!" Lucien laughed as he stumbled but it was cut off when Akira kissed him roughly. "Oh, I definitely look forward to more of this." He was slightly breathless after the kiss and went outside.

Akira and I worked together to make breakfast. He had a recipe for French toast from his mom that melted in your mouth. It had been a few months since he'd made it, we had had a Mass Effect 3 marathon that night. I had played my character and he had played his and we tried to see who could get farthest before we dropped from exhaustion. I lost because he's a werewolf, obviously, and could stay up for 48 hours without sleep easily. He made it as a peace offering when I threatened to throw his Xbox One outside and run it over a few times.

"Penny for your thoughts?" Akira bumped his shoulder to mine as he flipped a large piece of toast in the frying pan.

"I was just remembering our last video game marathon." I smile up at him. "Besides Lola, you are my best friend and now, you are one of the loves of my life. I'm so happy, even if this is a terrible situation, it brought all of us together." Now I was being all mushy and grabbed the dishes we would need.

"You're adorable." Akira finished making the last of the toast. "I love you too. And even though the detective hasn't said it, he probably feels the same. It might just take him awhile to admit it."

Lucien came back inside shortly after we set up the small breakfast buffet on the coffee table. He looked at the food and his stomach grumbled. I made him up a plate and watched him dig into it as he made appreciative noises every few bites. He must not get homemade food much. Akira and I would have to change that. I wanted it to be dinner time so I could make my favorite meal that I can cook for him.

"I received a call from my boss. Shane has some information for us about the staff you saw in your vision. He's expecting us in about an hour." Lucien leaned back after his last bite and sighed happily. "Akira, if I wasn't sleeping with you already, I would be after that."

Akira's chest rumbled in a chuckle as he picked up the dishes. "I'll wrap up the leftovers and put the dishes in the sink. I'll finish cleaning up when we come back from the meeting." His hips had a bit of a swagger as he walked away. Lucien's compliment went right to his head and when I looked over at Lucien, who was watching Akira's ass as he walked away, I smiled.

*W*e all rode in Lucien's car after a short argument with Akira. He wanted to take his truck and I said I had already driven it today and we needed to give Mother Earth a little break from it and use the car that used less gas. He griped about it but when we took a vote it was two to one and he lost. He'd always been a little bit of a sore loser, so he was quiet on the way to the MEPA office, his form of pouting.

"You know, Lucien, one thing is bugging me about your house, not that I'm not falling in love with it," Lucien took my hand as he opened my car door to help me out. "Your office is a chaotic mess, but from the parts I've seen, your house is spotless. How does that work?"

"I work better in my chaotic mess of an office." Lucien's lips curled and the fairy who flew past us made a sigh of appreciation at the sight. I eyed her and made sure she continued on. This one was mine. "My house is that clean because I pay a housekeeper to come in twice a week. You haven't seen my office in the house, though."

Akira walked on Lucien's other side and was looking around the courtyard as we approached his office. "This place is peaceful. Antihuman spell cast on the outside?" There were a couple of dwarves across the courtyard talking to a witch.

"Yes, there are only a few humans who work with us and are keyed to that spell and able to get in." We walked past his office. "We're going to go to the lab in the basement. Shane is waiting for us."

The door that we entered was layered in wards that were visible to the eye. They blazed bright neon colors, indicating that the wards were refreshed daily and extremely deadly.

"Not only is our lab down here," Lucien waved his hand over the wards and they deactivated, "so is the morgue and evidence locker." There were stairs that went down immediately from the door. Akira and I paused a few steps down and waited for Lucien who reactivated the wards on the door. "We have to ward this area to prevent theft, if someone even manages to get through our security, and to keep the evidence from trying to escape."

"The evidence? How can evidence escape?"

"A lot of evidence is magical in nature. Some of it has a mind of its own. Most of it is not dangerous but a couple are benevolent, so we have to take precautions. Shane is the one who is in charge of the evidence archives, which is why he is the expert to find out about that staff you saw."

The stairs finally ended and we entered a large circular room that had several doors lined along the walls. In the middle of the room stood equipment that looked like something out of a sci-fi novel. Two witches in white lab coats moved around the equipment, holding tubes of different types of liquids and there was a sharp cheddar smell in the air that it was making Akira's nose twitch.

Lucien muttered a word and the floor glowed briefly with a security spell that recognized his magic. He strode to the right and passed three doors before knocking on a blue door that seemed to be made of steel. The knock was unnaturally loud, a large echo carried throughout the room.

"Shane, it's us." Lucien yelled out. The blue door disappeared as if it had never been there and I had to look away and back to see if my eyes had been playing tricks on me. How cool was that?

Walking into the room was like being hit in the face with cold water. It was freezing and I loved it. This room was darker and not that large. Filing cabinets sat along the far wall and a single desk was on the right side of the room under a poster with a black cat looking regally down at people. The filing cabinets were large and there was some kind of shimmering light around them. Shane sat in the chair behind the desk scratching his beard.

"Ah! My favorite ghost handler!" He stood and his booming laugh filled the room. I had a feeling if he and Uncle Ray ever met, they would be good friends. "I was happy to hear that you were able to use that power your ghost gave you." He came over and I suddenly found myself with my feet dangling three feet in the air as he swung me around in a hug. "Welcome to my domain!" He sat me back down and shook Akira's hand as Lucien introduced them. "That staff you saw, it's an interesting relic." He gestured for us to sit as he went around his desk again as he jumped right in. Lucien stood between Akira and I behind the chairs.

Shane pulled out a large book that looked ancient from a small bookcase next to him. He placed it on his desk and opened the book about half way. The pages crinkled and looked like they were gold lined. He pointed to the page and the staff from my vision was in the lower right corner. Shane turned the book toward us so that we could see it. It was hand drawn but the grooves that I saw before were clearly there and the color was a deep red, almost black. It was beautiful and I reached forward, tracing the staff up to its pointed tip.

"This is most definitely it." I looked at the writing in the book. It almost looked like calligraphy, maybe it was. I wondered how old this book was, it was handwritten. "What is it?" I looked up at Shane. "It's obviously old."

"That's where this gets weird." Shane pointed to the writing that was under the picture. "This is a soul staff. They named it the Staff of Malum. It was first documented back when Jesus walked the world.

A powerful wizard created it to channel his magic, much like a summoning crystal, but this would be like a Mercedes to a Toyota." Shane flipped a couple of pages where another illustration of the staff took up the full page where it was more detailed, as if the staff could jump off the page. He ran a finger down the side of it, tracing the grooves.

"This staff was passed to the Wizard Guild for safe keeping in the 1600's. It was held by the leader of the guild for over 250 years when it was stolen. No one knows how or exactly when. The reason for its theft, though, was not a secret. Over the years, the leaders poured their magic into this staff, and because magic is a fickle thing, it became sentient."

Lucien hissed between his teeth. "That's never a good thing, especially when it's held by wizards."

Shane nodded. "From what I can decipher, the staff attracted negative energy after it was used to banish one of the last remaining demons who was still on this Earth." He turned the page and the staff was being held by a cloaked figure who looked familiar.

"That's the demon!" I jabbed a finger at the picture. "It has to be! The claws are the same!"

"It turns out, instead of banishing the demon, the demon's essence merged with the staff. Whoever possessed the staff would have the powers of the demon and," he looked at us seriously, "the demon was able to manifest thanks to the staff. No summoning required."

"That's why you didn't see the summoner in your vision, Vic." Lucien leaned forward, his eyes narrowing on the picture. "The staff allows the demon to walk on this Earth without another controlling it. Whoever has the staff, most likely, is the one pulling the strings. They can't be in their right mind if they are wielding this staff."

"So, this staff somehow has reappeared after hundreds of years and the demon is running around killing people who frequent Uncle Ray's bar? How does this make sense and why did the demon steal Siobal's summoning crystal if it's within this staff?"

"If the one who had the staff had a reason for it, the demon may have offered its services in exchange for whatever the demon wanted. What that is, is anyone's guess." Shane sounded like the idea was both fascinating and disturbing at the same time. My vote is just on disturbing and kind of disgusting the longer I thought about it. "As far as it taking that crystal? More power. I would have taken it too."

My phone vibrated in my pocket and I pulled it out to look at the text message that had come through. Akira leaned against my side to look at my phone with me and his face turned into a silent sneer. Shax had arrived in Gilbert and checked into a hotel. The text had multiple smiley faces and a kissy face with an eggplant after his message. I had to hold my phone away from Akira as he made to grab it as I replied with a generic response to Shax. We'd meet him in about two hours at the bar. I sent a text to Uncle Ray letting him know not to kill Shax if he got there before we got there.

"That's all I have for you, Lucien. I'll keep researching, I am trying to track down where it went after it was stolen." Shane stood, taking the book with him and went to the middle file cabinet on the back wall. He traced a small spell in the air that glowed above the cabinet and the wall parted in the middle.

My mouth dropped in awe as rows and rows of filing cabinets stretched for as far as the eye could see and beyond. I loved seeing magic in action. Shane flicked his fingers along and the cabinets raced like they were on a conveyor belt until they stopped and he placed the book inside one of the cabinets.

"Ghost girl, I hope the next time we see each other is under better circumstances." I got another hug before we left his room and the blue door snapped back into reality as soon as we walked out.

We went back up to Lucien's office and Akira's left eye began to twitch at the chaotic mess. I could see how he held himself back from trying to start cleaning up and that made me giggle. Akira was only a little OCD about cleaning. Lucien looked down at me and smiled, he probably figured out just by looking at Akira's posture what was bugging him but he didn't say anything to Akira. He was probably enjoying Akira's reaction as much as I was.

Lucien went to his desk and grabbed a few files that he glanced through briefly.

"The good news is that there have been no more victims. The bad news, even after combing Siobal's townhouse after the attack, there has been no leads from that end. With Shane researching and trying to track down where the staff's whereabouts have been, the best course of action right now is to see what your ex-boyfriend has to say about this and tomorrow we can see the rest of the other scenes." Lucien walked back over to me and gazed down into my eyes, barely inches away from me, "You are amazing and if not for you, this case would be flat lining." His hand cupped my cheek and I closed my eyes, leaning into it. His lips pressed against mine in a sweet kiss that lasted a few moments and felt like heaven.

"Oh, I really like when you do that." I let a sigh escape my lips as he pulled back and Akira snorted beside me. "I'll be happy to keep helping. I haven't seen Siobal since she helped with the vision, I should see if I can call her. Maybe she'll have more ideas." I felt a little bad. I hadn't thought about her since last night and I should have. Granted, she was dead and a ghost, but she had given me some of her powers to help catch this demon.

"Let's go get lunch and get to the bar. I'm about to go grab cleaning materials and clean this mess that Lucien calls an office." The gruff annoyed tone from Akira made Lucien and I laugh.

———

*W*e stopped at Chiles to get food and it was satisfying to watch the women and some men watch mine like they were desserts on a buffet and they were mine to partake of. We sat at a table since they wanted to sit next to me and a booth wouldn't hold both of them on one side and myself. Lucien kept his right arm across the back of my chair while Akira squeezed my thigh with his left hand. I'm pretty sure the waitress was planning my demise every time she came to the table.

"I think she wants to fuck you on this table." I dryly said to both of them as I took a bite of what remained of Lucien's cobb salad. "It's like I'm not even here."

Lucien's lips were wicked and he kissed my hand. "What do you care? We're the ones who are resisting throwing everything off of this table and fucking you witless."

I coughed in surprise as Akira's hand ran up to rub my upper thigh, causing heat to pool between my legs. My legs parted slightly on their own, the traitors. Lucien, not to be outdone, leaned against my side and his lips brushed along my neck and up to my ear.

"You both are evil." I hissed between my teeth as the waitress arrived, yet again, to the table.

"Can I get you any refills?" I swear she was puffing out her chest.

"We're good. The check would be great, though." Akira deepened his accent on purpose. "It's time we get back home and teach this filly a few moves from the Kamasutra."

The waitresses mouth dropped open, gaping like a fish, as she stuttered away.

Lucien and I were holding back our laughter and my face was buried in his neck as I fought to breath.

"You're so cruel." Lucien whispered to Akira in between his chuckles.

"What? It's true. At least, that's the plan after we go talk to dickweed at the bar."

That was it. I started laughing so hard I started to snort and that just made me laugh harder. The waitress came back and dropped the check on the table and stalked off, ignoring all of us. Akira threw three twenties next to the check and we left.

It only took a little over twenty minutes to get to the bar. We parked in the back in the employee parking and walked around the ally to the entrance. I noticed one of the bulbs for the two lights above the door was out and made a note to tell Uncle Ray. Humans couldn't see the lights because they were made of magical energy but we could. It was just a comfort thing, for the most part, letting the community know that the bar wouldn't have humans and you could come as you were.

Uncle Ray was sitting at one of the tables in the center of the bar. The table was littered with papers and maps. His third, Rick, sat across from him. Chase was behind the bar and it looked like he was reorganizing the alcohol. I would have to fix again later. These wolves always messing with my system.

"So, my favorite niece," Uncle Ray's voice thundered around the room, "you have that ex bastard coming to my bar?"

"Uncle Ray, you liked Shax until I broke up with him." I sat next to him and hugged him. "But, yes. The bar is familiar and the pack is here. Don't you think that's better with you here?" I raised my eyebrow at him.

"I liked him until he revealed what a snake he was." He returned my hug and gestured for Akira and Lucien to sit. "I have told the pack not to kill him when they see him. At least until after you're done with him. Then he's fair game." I shook my head at him and looked at my phone as it dinged. Shax was here and my stomach clenched and I felt like I was on the top of a roller coaster, waiting to drop.

I sucked in a breath as the bar door opened and he stepped through. It was like time had reversed. My heart skipped several beats and I had to swallow several times.

Shax had grown a little taller since the last time I had seen him. His body was lean, he must still run every morning. He'd cut his hair. It was so short the hair formed natural spikes. It was still the most beautiful dark red from my memories. His ears were still high on his head and pointed. His sharp angular eyes sparked light green, that flashed against the light. His smirk showed one of his longer than a human's canines and my mind flashed back to nights where he would use those teeth everywhere on me. He wore an expensive cream colored suit with a blue under shirt. I fought the blush that I knew was staining my cheeks.

Our eyes met and his smirk grew and he walked toward the table. "Vickie, you look beautiful." We all stood as he reached the table. "Ray, you're looking huge and intimidating. I see nothing has changed." His eyes moved over the others and stopped at Akira and he nodded, not fazed by Akira's threatening growl. When he made it to Lucien, he held out his hand. "You must be the detective that Vickie said is working the case."

Lucien's face was a pleasant professional mask as he took Shax's hand. "Detective Lucien. Thank you for coming to meet with us and your offer of help." He motioned to the table and Rick had pulled another chair for Shax, in between him and Akira. Lucien sat next to me and Uncle Ray was at the end of the table by himself.

"It's no trouble. My business practically runs itself now. I called my father and we discussed the vision that Vickie described to me." Shax was still cocky but right now he seemed to be behaving. "The staff," he began but Akira interrupted him.

"We know about the staff. MEPA has a book about it." If looks could kill, Shax would be a puddle of goo from the daggers coming from Akira's eyes.

"Interesting. So, you know that its sentient and houses a demon?" Lucien nodded to the question. "And you know the demon's name?" Silence was his answer. "I didn't think so."

Shax leaned forward and placed his hands on the table. "His name is Fa'gh and he is a demon parasite. My father found records of him that he passed along so I could share." He held one hand straight above the other. "Fa'gh is known for jumping from one demon host to the next, which made him a demon that even other demons despised and tried to kill."

I couldn't imagine why demons would take offense to another one of them hitching a ride and controlling them. Who wouldn't want that? It would be like a walk in the park.

Shax moved his hand higher. "When Fa'gh was banished from

the underworld, he was a blight on humanity." His hand curled as if he were imitating a spider. "He caused famine, death, and destruction wherever he went, even if his host was human. He earned the nickname, "Aranea", from the supernatural community. He is one of the reasons that the black plague spread and killed so many. It was a game to him." He pulled his hands back to a normal pose.

"A few hundred years later, most demons who were on Earth physically had been killed or sent back to the underworld, but not Fa'gh. The Wizards Guild hunted him for years until they caught him. They used the staff, which, by the way, is called Thu'onit, to kill him. At least, they thought they did. Turns out the staff just took Fa'gh into it, merging together, just like a parasite joining together with another parasite."

"So, we have a name. What does that do to help?" Rick spoke quietly. He was a large man and didn't speak often.

"Having a demon's name will let us trap him in a circle when you catch him. Once he's trapped, he can be permanently killed. That's what I can help with."

"You can kill the demon? I thought it was almost impossible to do that." My question is what was probably going through everyone's mind. "How?"

Shax focused his green eyes on me and I had to swallow. My body was shameful and I fought the memories that kept wanting to pop up.

"I have a dagger, something only a demon bloodline can use. My father overnighted it to me when I called him. It will be at my hotel by the time this meeting is over."

"That seems awfully convenient, having a demon killing dagger on hand." Uncle Ray wasn't being subtle about not liking Shax.

"My family has always been known for our demon bloodline. We aren't ashamed of it. Obviously, you need that dagger to help kill this demon. So, I would say it's a good thing my family isn't afraid to embrace our evil side, wouldn't you?"

And now Shax was purposely trying to piss the shifters off by pissing Uncle Ray off. I had just opened my mouth to change the subject but Lucien beat me to it.

"On behalf of the Arizona branch of MEPA, we thank you for your assistance and will be grateful for any additional assistance you provide."

Shax leaned back in his chair, his legs spread out relaxed. "I came here for Vickie."

I watched as a tick flicked along Lucien's mouth, the first sign of any annoyance from him. "Regardless, thank you." He handed Shax his card. "We are still looking into tracking this Fa'gh down so that we can capture him. When we do, we will need you and your dagger to stop him. Headquarters gave the go ahead last week to kill this killer when he was caught."

"No due process within the magical community." Shax chuckled softly. "I would expect no less." He put Lucien's card in his pocket of his shirt. "I would like a few minutes alone with Vickie."

All three of the shifters pushed back their chairs and stood, but not because they were going, they looked ready to pummel Shax. I stood and placed my hand on Akira's chest.

"It was part of the deal. He'd help us and I would talk to him alone. It's ok." I smiled up at Akira. "It's not like he can hurt me again." I could have sworn I saw Shax flinch but it was gone within a second.

Uncle Ray clapped Akira on the shoulder and gestured to Rick. They walked over to the bar and after a quick kiss from Akira, he joined them. Lucien followed after he reached out to squeeze my hand. Shax watched them with a calculating gaze.

"So," I sat across from him, "what did you want to talk about?"

Shax pulled out a white card that had a spell of silence on it. He placed it in the middle of the table and said the activation word. A white sheen arched over the table ensuring our conversation was private.

"I see some things have changed since you left me." Shax went back to reclining in the chair. "I'm not surprised you're with Akira, but the detective too? That's not something I ever suspected you would be interested in."

I shook my head. "You didn't come all the way from Nevada to talk about my love life, Shax."

"Oh, but I did." He narrowed his eyes. "I want to know the reason for our breakup. You never even talked to me. You used the pack to push me away. I never thought of you as a coward until that moment."

It felt like he had reached across the table and slapped me. My face must have shown the shock I felt because Akira was two steps off the bar stool before I motioned for him that it was alright. Taking a deep breath, I met Shax's gaze.

"I'm not the one who broke us up. I heard you when you were on the phone with your dad. You told him you were going to break up with me soon and that I was just a passing fling you kept around because it was easier stringing along one girl instead of several."

It took a few seconds but Shax nodded as he recalled the phone call I had overheard. "And instead of talking to me about the conversation, and finding out why I said that to my father, you assumed the worst and wrote me off. Five years together and you didn't even give me the courtesy of listening to my side before you broke things off." His face and voice were flat and I couldn't tell what he was feeling.

He did have a point. I hadn't given him the option to talk to me. I had hidden behind Uncle Ray and Akira for weeks. I had basically turned my phone off after he wouldn't stop blowing it up with texts and voicemails.

"Alright. What's your side of the story?"

A grim half smile appeared. "Oh, no. It's not going to be that easy. You owe me. Dinner at my hotel tonight. I assume you'll have your lovers with you. They can make use of the hotels pool or whatever while you and I talk and eat in my room. You owe me that much. And you can tell the detective that Fa'gh wouldn't dare attack you while you're with me because of the dagger. It will alert me when other demon blood is nearby."

He stood and picked up the card with the silence spell. It faded away as he put it away. "I'll text you the hotel I am staying at and the time dinner will be served. See you in a few hours." He waved at the shifters and walked out of the bar as if it hadn't been five years since he had last stepped inside of it.

Uncle Ray beat Akira and Lucien to the table and took my hand. "You ok, dove?" His eyes were furrowed in concern and I patted his hand.

"I think so. He wants closure. He made a few good points. I didn't handle our break up very well and the relationship deserved better." I looked up at the three of them. "We're going to have dinner and, hopefully, that will be the end of it." Famous last words.

CHAPTER 11

*A*kira wasn't happy with the arrangement but Lucien and I were able to convince him that attacking Shax and ripping his arms off wasn't in our best interest.

"I might not like it," Lucien had reasoned, "but he is here for a reason. He has a way of killing the demon. We need his help or he wouldn't have been part of Vickie's vision. We are going to be in the same building, and if I'm being honest, with the power he was hiding, Vickie will be perfectly safe with him."

That had been a surprise. I had never wondered about Shax's power, even when we were in school. I hadn't cared and he hadn't cared about mine. It shouldn't have surprised me, though. Shax had two demon bloodlines. His mother had been a third ice demon and his father was a third earth demon. He had never gone over how powerful his parents were but with the power Lucien apparently felt, it had to be high.

"So, while Vickie is being wined and dined, we can take advantage of the hot tub, what do you say?" Lucien winked at Akira and that helped bring him out of the bad mood he had been in since seeing Shax.

"I guess we can go in the hot tub for a little while." He grumbled softly as he eyed Lucien like he was a candy apple, his favorite dessert. "Maybe scare off any annoying humans."

Men. Promise of sexy time and their moods instantly improved. I was a little sad I would miss watching them in a hot tub but I had made a deal. We stopped at my studio to pick up some more clothes after I had complained that the shirts Akira had picked were not dinner appropriate.

Both pairs of eyes had looked down at my chest for several seconds and I had to snap my fingers at them to look back up. They had agreed I should wear something different. I grabbed a few new shirts, pants, and a dress for tonight.

We were able to spend two hours relaxing at Lucien's when I got the text from Shax. He was staying at one of the casinos and it was only a twenty minute car ride if we got on the 202. The room number he gave me had to be one of the rooms higher up and he sent another text letting us know that the hotel was aware that Akira and Lucien would be using the amenities and Lucien whistled.

"It's not the cheapest place to stay. I've been there a few times for work. It's a nice casino but the swimming pool and hot tub are for hotel guests only, so he must have some pull if we get to swim without any issues."

I rubbed the back of my neck. "You guys know that nothing's going to happen, right? I love you two and this is only for closure and I hold to my promises."

Akira had yanked me into his arms and had given me a crushing kiss that left me weak kneed and he had just handed me over to Lucien who had repeated the action. They were trying to kill me with their kisses. It wasn't a bad way to go.

"We know and we trust you." Lucien let me go and nudged me to the bedroom. "Go ahead and get changed." I realized I had told Lucien I loved him for the first time but he hadn't said it back. I wasn't sure how to feel about that. I probably shouldn't have said it considering this was new but I don't like to lie to myself.

It only took a few minutes to strip out of my shirt and jeans and into the simple black dress I had grabbed out of my closet. It was sleeveless but had a tall neck and fell to my knees. It hugged my curves in a way that was classy. I put on a pair of one inch black heels, brushed my hair out so that it fell around my shoulders, a tiny bit of lip gloss and I was ready. I figured getting all made up for Shax wouldn't be a good idea for any party involved.

When I went back into the living room Akira was giving a lecture to Lucien about cleaning up. Apparently, he had seen Lucien's office in the house and had not been pleased. Lucien sat there with a bemused expression as he listened to Akira gripe at him. When he saw me, he stood though, and nudged at Akira.

"It's not fancy but it should suffice for a simple dinner?" I pulled the skirt and swished it around my knees.

"Go change back into a shirt and jeans. He's not allowed to see you like this." Akira growled and his eyes flashed with heat. If I wasn't careful, we weren't going to leave the house.

I decided it was better to play it off. "You're a dork, Akira. Let's go. We're going to be late." I grabbed my phone and purse and walked out the front door. Akira's curses followed me but it was only a few moments later that they both were outside. Akira carried a gym bag that had their swim trunks and we got into his truck. I wasn't going to battle him over taking the car when the hotel was only twenty minutes away.

"You look radiant." Lucien whispered to me from the backseat and I smiled over my shoulder at him. "Akira's just being overprotective. You're probably used to it by now."

That made Akira stutter in mock anger. "Overprotective? Me? How dare you!" They went back and forth as we drove to the hotel and by the time we arrived, we were all laughing again and more relaxed.

It was a busy evening already, then I remembered that it was Friday. When we went into the hotel, I was a little dazzled from how it was decorated. It was modern and welcoming at the same time. It only took a few minutes before the guys had to go a different way than I.

"I'll text you when I'm heading down?" I pushed the button to the top floor of the hotel.

"Yes, we'll keep both of our phones with us." Lucien smile was slightly pained. "I don't like it either, but you need to have that closure and Akira can easily rip him apart if he makes you cry." Akira grinned at the idea excitedly.

I snorted as I got into the elevator. "Go have some fun, you two. I'll see you in an hour or so." The doors closed and I was on my way up. No one else was going up so my elevator ride only took a minute to get to the top. Shax was waiting as the door opened. He was wearing a navy blue suit with a crème under shirt this time.

"Victoria." He took my hand and kissed it. The old familiar fire rushed up my arm. "You make simple elegance breathtaking." He had gotten a lot smoother with his words these past years.

"Thank you. I see you went from jeans to suits. Moving up in the corporate world?"

Shax opened the door to his suite and we stepped into a room that had to be the presidential suite. The room had several comfortable looking couches, a separate dining room, and a guest bathroom before it led into the bedroom, but I wasn't going anywhere near that part of the suite.

"I opened a small restaurant in Vegas that offered entertainment for both of the sexes. It's done well so I'm thinking of expanding." Shax went over to one of the couches and sat down, his right leg crossing over his left. "I ordered dinner. It should be here momentarily." He was acting stiff, formal, and not at all like the Shax I remembered.

I put my hands on my hips and faced him. "Why are you acting like such a stick in the mud? Since when do you wear suits and act like money is everything." I gestured, taking in the whole suite we stood in.

Shax shook his head and ran a hand through his hair. "Look, it's been years since we last saw each other. I have always cared about money. I grew up in a household of money and responsibility was beaten into me. You would know that if we had talked about my past more." He wasn't holding back his punches at all today. "I like making money and spending it."

"Is it my fault that you choose to be closed off about your life? No matter how many years we were together you never wanted to talk about your family."

A knock sounded from the door and interrupted our conversation. Shax stood to open the door and I muttered, "This conversation is far from over." And that caused Shax to laugh as he stepped aside for the waiter to wheel in a cart that was covered in trays of food.

Shax moved to the dining room off to the side and the waiter followed. He held out a chair for me but I decided to be difficult and sat in a different one. That just seemed to amuse him more, though, and he sat in the chair. The waiter served the food quickly and quietly. Shax handed him a tip and promised to leave the trays outside the room when we were done eating.

"I hope you still like steak?" His tone was dry as he cut into his steak. "That can't have changed much. You always took steak over anything else but you couldn't make one to save your life."

"I'm just not good at cooking. There are plenty of other people around that are." I cut into my steak, it was like carving into butter. I wouldn't look at Shax as I took a bite and had to hold back a moan. It was delicious. I wasn't going to tell him that, though. He'd probably take it as a compliment of his skill to order steak or something.

"Look," after a few bites I decided to continue the conversation, "what we had is in the past. We both screwed up. I should have told you what I overheard so you could explain yourself. We could have worked on our communication skills overall thinking back on it."

Shax gazed at the wall beside him before speaking. "I think you're right on that." He sighed and suddenly he was the Shax I remembered and not this façade he had created. "Look, V, when you left me it really messed me up. I've tried for years to figure out why you just left and wouldn't talk to me." He ran his hands through his hair, he tended to do that when he was frustrated. "I'm sorry you heard that conversation I had with my father. I wish you had confronted me instead of running so I could have explained."

He stood and removed his jacket then loosened his shirt sleeves, rolling them up to his elbows, his muscles were clearly defined and my mouth watered at the sight. "My father never wanted me to have the independence I had while we were together. I lived away from him and had my own life. But I still had to report back to him if he was going to pay for school."

He came around the table and pulled the chair next to me out and sat in it, facing me. "V, I loved you with everything I was. You were always on my mind, even if we were apart. We fit together perfectly but my father had always controlled my life. He had sold me to the highest bidder when I was five in the ruse of an arranged marriage."

That was news to me. We had been together for five years and I wasn't kidding when he never said anything about his family or past. In hindsight, I was pretty naive and the blame couldn't be put squarely on his shoulders anymore.

"That night, just like anytime I spoke with my father, I lied to him. It was just easier to placate him about our relationship than deal with him. I was using him for his money. That might sound crass, but my family has always been about the bottom line and mine was finishing college and being with you even if that wasn't his plan for me."

I wanted to be mad at him for the way he acted with his dad but I couldn't, I felt sad because we both seem to have come from some messed up parenting. At least I had Uncle Ray but Shax was on his own.

"I'm sorry." We both spoke at once and laughed as we realized we had said the same thing.

"Thank you for helping with this demon." I patted his hand gently before picking up my knife and fork to keep eating. "Tell me about your business that sounds like a fancy strip joint." I grinned at him. "Because that's what it is, right?"

Just like that, we were talking like we used to. Shax insisted his restaurant was classier and more of a burlesque show rather than a strip joint. Not that I had anything against strippers. I just hated how coordinated they were when they danced and their legs were usually perfect. I usually looked like I was chicken legged and stepping on Legos in the middle of the night when I tried to dance.

It wasn't long before an hour had come and gone. We finished dessert and I texted Akira that I was going to head down in a few minutes. I faced Shax for the first time in years with a smile.

"This was good. I'm glad we cleared the air. I'll give Lucien your number and you guys can work out the details when we find the demon?"

"I'll talk to him, yeah. I had a few ideas that I'll run by him in the morning." Shax held the door open for me and I slid past him but he pressed close as I did. Our bodies brushed sending fire racing through my limbs. "I'll talk to you in the morning."

I hid the shiver he caused as well as I could and stepped into the elevator. His green eyes and his smirk stayed with me as the floors went past. I was in love with Akira and Lucien. We had literally just had sex for the first time a few days ago. I was not going to ruin a good thing thinking about my ex-boyfriend and what could have been.

———

*B*oth Akira and Lucien looked comfortable and sated when we met down stairs. My lips quirked and I suspected that they may have enjoyed each other's company a little more than the average guest. I sure hoped they did, although I wanted to watch. Maybe I could convince them to let me watch when we got home.

That thought had me wanting to skip to the truck. I spun around toward them and walked backwards with my hands clasped behind me. Akira chuckled as he walked by me to get to the truck first so he could open the door like the Texan gentleman he was.

"So, you obviously enjoyed yourselves." I drawled, imitating Akira's accent.

"You're a brat and not funny." Akira snorted as he unlocked the truck and held open the door for me to climb in. He managed to get a grope of my ass as I crawled across the passenger seat.

"Hey!" I laughed and swatted backwards at him but I ended up smacking Lucien in the chest as he got in next to me. "Sorry, Lucien. I was aiming for Akira."

Lucien just shook his head laughing along with me as we buckled ourselves in. Akira got in on the driver's side and we headed back to Lucien's.

"Tomorrow, we will go over the rest of the crime scenes, after I check in at the office, and do more research into this staff." Lucien put their bags into the back of the crew cab. "We're close, I can almost taste it."

"You sure it's not something else you taste?" Akira flashed a smirk over at Lucien.

"You two better not have gone all the way, yet. I want to watch." Looking between the two, I narrowed my eyes.

Lucien snorted. "No, I just sucked him off." He winked at me as my face flushed even though heat grew between my legs at just the image that produced. "You can watch tonight." He placed his hand on my inner thigh and squeezed. He had to know he was being a tease and I glared at him for a second before looking back to Akira.

"Hurry up and get us home."

"As the lady wishes." Akira got us home in record time even as he adhered to the laws of the road. We basically raced each other inside, laughing and pulling at each other's clothes.

I'm not sure why it felt like there was some kind of urgency, but that feeling was there just waiting to burst. I was the first one naked and I helped Akira throw off Lucien's clothes as we stumbled into his bedroom and onto the bed in a clash of limbs. Lucien lay on my right side, his lips were locked with mine, his tongue plunging in and taking over. His fingers traced circles around my nipples making them ache and strain to be touched.

"Oh, gods," I gasped into his mouth, my hands were in his hair, "would you stop teasing already?" The only answer was his mouth traveling down my neck and his thumbs flicking my nipples at the same time making my back arch into his hands. "You're both jerks!" I gritted my teeth as my pussy clenched in pleasure with just these touches from him.

"Oh, darlin', you know you love us." Akira was behind Lucien; his hand was stroking Lucien's side and up to his chest. "Here. I'll help give you some revenge." His voice deepened and he pinched Lucien's left nipple making him gasp. "The detective here is so sweet."

Akira was pressing kisses along the back of his neck. His hand stroked downward over Lucien's abs and I watched with heavy eyes as Akira took Lucien's cock in his hand and started to stroke him, squeezing as he twisted his hand up and down. Lucien moaned as his head slumped forward to rest on my chest as his hips jerked slightly with Akira's rhythm.

That was so hot and we hadn't even gotten started. I watched as Akira stroked Lucien's cock to the point where he was panting and about to come when Akira pulled his hand away. Lucien whipped his head over his shoulder to glare at Akira and Akira just chuckled pleasantly.

"Don't worry, bubble butt. I'm going to make you come so hard that you'll want to pass out. But, first," Akira pushed Lucien so that he was straddling me, his arms braced next to my head, "we can't forget our Vickie." Akira rolled off the bed, and I heard the nightstand drawer open and shut after a few seconds. He reappeared and knelt behind Lucien and I heard him open the top of a bottle.

Lucien growled back at Akira but I decided I wanted to be included in this so I reached down with both hands and started stroking Lucien's cock and gently tugging on his balls. A rumble in his chest made my pussy even hotter and his lips sealed over my right nipple with teeth and tongue. At this point I might have my orgasm without being touched.

Akira, not to be out done, with his fingers covered in lube, started pressing two fingers inside of Lucien and his cock quivered in my touch as Akira slowly started to get him ready for his cock.

"Damn, baby, you're tight. Gotta let me in." Akira purred softly as he leaned over Lucien's back and kissed his shoulder. I watched over Lucien's shoulder as Akira twisted and worked three fingers inside of him and Lucien moved his mouth from one nipple to the next, getting rougher with his teeth. He pulled back slightly and kissed my lips, biting my lower lip.

"Hurry up, Akira. I'm about to burst." He gritted his teeth as he hissed even as he gently pushed my hands away from his cock. "Has he always been this much of a tease?" He didn't give me a chance to reply before he was thrusting inside of me. I cried out as he stretched my pussy and my arms wrapped around his shoulders.

"I'm always going to tease my loved ones." Akira's voice was gruff and he clutched Lucien's hips to hold him still, and I could feel Lucien's cock throbbing inside of me.

Akira looked into my eyes and thrust inside of Lucien. I couldn't see where they joined but Lucien's face scrunched up for a second before Akira pulled back and slammed into him which caused him to thrust inside of me.

Lucien and I both cried out as Akira started to pull back and thrust again. Lucien moaned as he lay on top of me, holding himself up slightly by his elbows. His eyes were closed and at each thrust a small moan or gasp escaped his lips. Akira must be hitting his prostate at each thrust because I could feel Lucien pulling back inside of me to push up into Akira's thrust that just forced Lucien harder inside of me.

It wasn't long before I lost all sense of time. It was all I could do to cling to Lucien as Akira took over and fucked both of us at a pace a marathon runner would be jealous of. I had already come once by the time Akira's panting became more rapid. Their thighs met roughly and the constant push and pull made the mattress squeak and the headboard sounded a crack each time Akira slammed into us. His thrusts became erratic and I clenched around Lucien as they both cried out, or roared in Akira's case, and came at the same time. I clenched around Lucien as his warmth filled inside of me and I came again seeing stars. They both fell forward on top of me for several seconds before Akira rolled over to the left and Lucien rolled to the right. I felt slightly empty as he pulled out and cool air touched my body.

"Holy Gods." Lucien murmured into his pillow. "You both are going to be the death of me."

"Ah, but it'll be a satisfied one, no?" Akira was smug as he got out of bed and came back after a few minutes with a towel and wet wipes. I took a wipe from him to clean myself and watched as he tenderly helped Lucien. I knew I'd feel this in the morning.

My heart had never felt as complete as it did at this moment. We had a demon serial killer to catch but we had found each other in this crazy situation. The world continued to move on its axis as we cleaned up after sex, but it felt like time had paused just for a few moments, to allow us to be happy.

CHAPTER 12

"So, we go to your office and afterward we visit the remaining crime scenes to see if any of the other ghosts can give information we don't already have?"

We were finishing our breakfast the next morning after a bit of playtime in the bathtub. I was trying my best not to drag them back to bed; we had to catch the killer before there was another victim.

"Change of plans," Lucien finished his coffee and started to braid his hair, "I got a text from Shane. With that information from your vision, he thinks they've narrowed down the warehouse location. Shane wants to show you a few pictures and see if you recognize any of the locations. After, my team and I are going to go hunting with Shax and his dagger. You and Akira will come back here for safety."

"Change of plans? When did you get the text? And we aren't going to hide while you hunt this guy down." I scoffed at him. "That's not how this works."

"Vickie," he finished his hair and placed a hand over mine and squeezed. "This is my job. You have to let me do it. I can't be worrying about you or Akira when I'm with my team and we are hunting this guy. You've done enough, let me catch this guy so we don't have to worry about him hurting you somehow. Let Akira do his job of protecting you away from potentially dangerous situations, okay?"

Oh, he was sneaky. It wasn't fair to use logic in a fight. That's not how it was supposed to go. I wanted to argue but he made a good point. Plus, if I was there and they did find the demon it wasn't like I could help if there was a fight. I relented and sighed.

"Fine." I mumbled and grabbed the dishes from the table. "You're right."

"How badly did that hurt to admit?" Akira grinned over at me as he was getting his keys.

"Shut up," I glared at him as we all moved to the garage. "I just don't like it."

"I promise that I'll take every precaution I can." Lucien stopped by me and kissed me gently. "With any luck, we'll catch this guy and this will finally be over." He got into his car as Akira got into his truck. I hopped into the car and off we went.

---

*S*hax was leaning against a black Lexus with his arms crossed, not looking like he was bothered by the heat and humidity. He was also decked out in leather pants with a large belt that had a large dagger strapped to it and a blue wife beater. A smile bloomed across his face as he saw us get out of the vehicles. I had to remind myself to take a breath and ignore those past feelings that kept rearing their ugly heads. Back down hydra, it is not your time.

"You look gorgeous." His voice was low as he stepped forward to hug me but was sidelined when Akira stepped in front of me and received the hug instead. I couldn't tell who was more traumatized, Akira or Shax.

I laughed as Shax jumped back and started brushing his arms like he had ants. Akira just glared and his mouth was a silent snarl.

"You're both very pretty. Let's get out of this heat, please." I tossed over my shoulder as I followed Lucien. They shared a glare then followed us. I had to hold back another laugh as they sped-walked to catch up to us as if it were a race.

We went down to the evidence room again and the circular forensics lab still gave me the shivers as we went around it. Shane was at his desk when we entered and the room soon felt even smaller with the other three men crowding it.

"My ghost girl!" Shane's huge smile and white teeth flashed. "You're just who I need to go over these warehouses that fit the vision description." He raised an eyebrow at the other men. "Quite an entourage you've acquired."

I gestured toward Shax who was looking at the filing cabinets with interest. "This is Shax. He's agreed to help us. You remember Akira."

Shane nodded at them and he motioned for me to sit across from him. "Let's get to the point. The longer this demon is around, the more victims will pile up. And, quite frankly, I'm tired of all this overtime. I'd like to see my wife for more than a few minutes a day."

"You're married?" I probably shouldn't have asked that in such a surprised tone. "Not that that's bad!" Nice save, Vickie.

"That was smooth." Siobal appeared next to Shane with her signature smirk on her face. "Insult the guy who helped you with my powers."

"Siobal! I was wondering where you had gone to. I was starting to get worried."

Her smirk turned into a shy smile. "I didn't mean to. I figured you didn't need me at this point so I started following this guy. I've gotten to talk to Spirit a few times. It's been interesting."

I glanced at Shane and back to Siobal. "Can Shane see you?"

"No." She shook her head. "You're the only one who can see ghosts that's not an Elemental. You're special, Victoria. You need to start believing that."

I felt my face heat and glanced away from her only to meet

Shax's eyes. The gentle green was a comfort from years past and I had to look away before memories overtook me again. Damn hydra.

Shane and Lucien were speaking quietly while I had been having my conversation with Siobal. It was nice that I could talk to her, a ghost, and not be considered strange or demented by these guys. And that they gave me time to talk to the ghost? That was kind of sweet.

"Alright, let's have a look at the warehouses and their locations on the map." Shane pulled out a folder that was filled with pictures from what looked like satellite photos and blueprints. He pulled up Google maps on his computer and swiveled the monitor to face me.

"So, first one I pulled up is in the city of Maricopa. It's on the far edges and used to be a tractor shed." He did air quotes when he said shed. "It's fairly large but hasn't been in use for a few years." He pushed a photo of a building toward me and pulled up the address on the monitor.

"Concentrate on the warehouse in your vision." Siobal spoke up. "Empty your thoughts except for the warehouse when you look at the pictures and map. That should help you. You'll know if it's the place, trust me."

I was beginning to see a pattern with these powers. Clear my mind except for the end goal and hope it works. I know the guys were giving me a weird look as I giggled slightly but I closed my eyes after committing the information in front of me to memory and started focusing on what I was seeking. As I focused more, I started to glow again. My new powers in action. I would have to ask Siobal if glowing was normal or if it was a side effect from Spirit.

We went through seven warehouses with no luck. The first three were out in the middle of nowhere and hadn't given me any kind of inkling. The last four were more city bound but didn't stir any kind of recollection. Shane had three more prospects before he would have to go back to searching for more warehouses.

The eighth one was an abandoned plane hangar that was used as a storage warehouse that was out near the Mesa Gateway airport. My stomach filled with butterflies and as my fingers touched the satellite photo there was a small tingle, as if there was a message that was saying we were close but not yet there.

"This isn't it but," my brows furrowed, "it's close to here. This area," I dragged a finger around the small airport and the surrounding area until the tingle disappeared, "he's near here." It felt right as I said it.

"Perfect." Shane took back the pictures and pulled the monitor around to face him as he started typing quickly. "I'll get the surveys of that area and meet you upstairs, Lucien."

Lucien was already walking out the door and I scrambled out of my seat to follow him with Akira and Shax right behind me. Lucien was on his cell phone as we went around the forensics lab and up the stairs. He was barking orders at whoever was on the other end of the phone. He turned toward us as we got to the inner courtyard with a grim expression but I could tell he was bursting with energy.

"I'm rounding up anyone we can spare and we are going to sweep the area that you mentioned, Vic. It's not a large area but it's going to take some time to go through it without raising any human suspicion." He placed his hands on my shoulders and grinned down at me. "You are amazing." He placed a brief kiss on my lips before striding away toward his office. Akira and I looked at each other and scoffed gently. Lucien was pretty hot when he got serious.

"Shax," Lucien called over his shoulder as we followed him into his office, "we're going to need you and your dagger on this hunt tonight."

Shax nodded and he pulled out said dagger with his right hand and I wanted to take a closer look. It was the size of his forearm. It looked to be made of black stone, the grip was wood and looked worn and ancient. He ran his index and middle fingers of his left hand down the flat side of the dagger. "I'm ready. It'll be a relief to get rid of this parasite once and for all."

"Vic and I will head out and lock ourselves up at your place, Lucien." Akira grabbed my hand and squeezed it. "Just like we talked about."

I sighed, frustrated, but nodded in agreement. "Yeah, yeah. Just promise to check in with us and be safe, ok?" I hugged Lucien and he pulled me tightly into his arms. I felt his lips press against my temple. I pulled back so that Akira could have a moment and I went to stand in front of Shax.

Shax smiled at me and it was devoid of any snark, he was being sincere when he smiled at that moment. I reached out and hugged him quickly before stepping back and ignored the feelings that bloomed in my chest at the touch.

"Be safe, ok?" I offered him my own smile. "Don't do anything reckless."

I saw a hint of his fangs as he bowed with a flourish. "As my lady commands."

I snorted as Akira and I left Lucien's office. I refused to look back. A horrible churning in my stomach had started and I didn't want to run back into Lucien's office to demand he stay behind. I had to trust him. We climbed into Akira's truck and started toward Lucien's house.

"He'll be fine. They'll do their jobs and catch this guy. Shax'll get rid of him and we can go back to our normal lives, together." Akira spoke softly as we turned onto a frontage road and he squeezed my hand. "It'll be fine."

CHAPTER 13

There was an annoying sound, like someone was eating some mushy cereal right in my ear. I groaned as I tried to go back to sleep. The sound just kept going on and it was getting annoying.

"Akira, stop chewing and swallow. That sound is gross." I grumbled into my hard and dusty pillow.

Wait. Hard and dusty? That didn't sound right. I forced my eyes to open, they felt heavy and it hurt when the faded sunlight hit them. I had to squint for a minute to get my bearings. I wasn't in Lucien's bed, that was the only thing I was able to process at that moment.

As my eyes started to clear, I found that I was looking up into a high industrial ceiling. That wasn't right. When did I go to one of the warehouses with Lucien? I left the MEPA office before Lucien and his team were ready to go. I tried to wipe at my eyes but my arms wouldn't move. That was weird, they felt like they were pressed to my sides tightly and I couldn't move them and there was a pressure and jolt of pain when I tried on my right side. Maybe I fell when we were looking at the warehouse?

But that wasn't right. I shook my head, trying to clear my

thoughts and I noticed that sound again. The chewing of old mushy cereal. I glance to my left and that's when reality crashed in on me like a semi-truck.

I wasn't in the truck or Lucien's bed. I was in a warehouse but no one was with me except the person making that disgusting noise. I was staring at Fa'gh, the demon parasite. My blood turned to ice and I started to shiver even though it had to be over a hundred degrees in the warehouse.

He was still in that ridiculous cloak that hid most of his features but I could see his mouth and sharp teeth clearly as he chewed on something. He watched me from where he lounged in the chair from my vision. He was holding that plastic bag and there were only three eyeballs left in it. That had to be what he was eating and making that sound. His eyes practically glowed within the hood. It was the first time seeing them, and I wished I hadn't. They looked similar to a goat's eye, slanted pupils, and the color was a bright red that reminded me of blood.

"So, you finally wake up." The voice was like nails on a chalkboard. "You've been out for almost a whole day. When I hit your truck, I didn't expect you to be so weak. Had to give you some of my blood to keep you alive."

"What do you mean?" My voice was scratchy and my throat felt parched. "You hit the truck?" It felt fuzzy, the memory that was trying to surface. "What do you mean?"

Fa'gh cursed and he slammed his hands onto the table in front of him. "Don't you dare tell me you don't remember anything! He will be displeased if you don't scream and recognize him as you die."

Fa'gh had to be eating some rancid eyeballs. I had no idea who "he" was, and I had an inkling I really didn't want to find out. I did want to remember about the truck, though. The memory was pushing against my mind and I knew something was important to remember but it was still fuzzy to grasp.

I closed my eyes, trying to ignore the raging temper tantrum that the demon was throwing in front of me. I thought back on what I last remembered.

We were at the MEPA office and I was trying to help them narrow down this idiot's location. Siobal was there with Shane when we went into his office. Lucien started ordering his team about getting ready to search for Fa'gh. I was supposed to go to his house and stay safe with...who was I supposed to be with? That's where it got fuzzy. I hadn't been driving the truck because it wasn't my vehicle. Whose was it?

That's when it came flooding back. Akira. Akira had been driving the truck and was with me when we left the MEPA office. We had been on the frontage road about to pull onto the highway when a large tow truck had slammed into us from the right side.

I remembered the loud crunching of metal, my screams, Akira's shouts, the smell of burnt oil and rubber. The passenger side door had caved in and I remembered looking down at a large piece of glass from the windshield through my right side.

I had reached for Akira's hand when Fa'gh had wrenched open the driver's side and his right hand had pierced through Akira's chest; his black claws had been covered in his blood. Akira's eyes had dulled and gone blank as the claws had shredded his heart before Akira was able to react. Just like that, the man who I had loved for almost half of my life was gone.

Tears fell as I remembered Akira was killed and thrown over Fa'gh's shoulder into the street. Fa'gh had reached over to me and all I felt was searing pain. I had passed out as I had tried to punch at him and get away. I opened my eyes to glare at the demon who had caused so much pain.

"You disgusting parasite!" I managed to spit out without crying at the pain of watching Akira being killed. "I will kill you if it's the last thing I do!"

Fa'gh paused in his temper tantrum of throwing things around and swung around to look down at me.

"So, you remembered." He sounded happy. "That's good! That

means he can kill you with your memory intact and I will finally have fulfilled my contract with him." Fa'gh ran his claws down his face. "I can't wait to be free and kill who I want, when I want."

I tried to sit up and realized I was tied down with a rope around my middle and my arms were behind my back. When I tried to move, there was a sharp pain in my right side again and I remembered what Fa'gh had said a little bit earlier about how he had to give me blood to keep me alive. I felt myself pale and I fought the urge to throw up on my empty stomach.

"How did you keep me alive?" I had to focus. If I could keep him distracted long enough, maybe Lucien and Shax would find us and put an end to him. And if I focused on getting away from him, I wouldn't think of Akira. "How did you know where to find me?"

"Like I said," Fa'gh sounded bored as he sat back down in the chair and threw his legs up on the table, "I had to give you some of my blood. Demon blood is almost like Angel's blood to other races. It helped heal your internal wounds enough to keep you alive." He burped and I had to fight again to keep from throwing up. "I was surprised how fast you healed though. Most humans, that's really what you are isn't it? Anyway, most humans don't heal quickly, even with the boost of our blood." He leaned forward to glare at me. "I would have had your soul by now if you hadn't managed to take away my demon mark. And to how I found you? Easy. I watched the MEPA office. Stupid idiots have been searching everywhere for me but I've been right in front of them."

Swallowing back the bile that had risen in my throat, I tried to process what he had said. He had used his blood to keep me alive but I was still going to be killed by him soon enough. I needed to figure out who this "he" was. It had to be the man who found the staff that Fa'gh is trapped in and made a contract. Finding out where I was being held prisoner was probably up there on the list of good things to do.

Fa'gh leaned back again and opened up the Ziploc bag and

grabbed one of the remaining eyeballs. He held it between two claws and squinted at it.

"These are getting too old. I need to get some fresh ones." He popped the eyeball in and chewed with his mouth open. I tried to keep the sound out of my head but it was a haunting sound.

"Where are we?"

Fa'gh glances at me again but keeps chewing. "Somewhere close to the freeway. He'll be here soon, guess it doesn't matter if you know that." He snorted amused by his wit and stared at his boots.

"Are we near the airport?"

He just looked at me but one of his eyes gave a slight twitch and I knew I was right. If I could find a way to tell Lucien where we were, I might just survive this encounter. I decided to try to ignore him and think on how I could get away or help Lucien find this place. I glanced around and took in the metal ceiling, cement floors, and stucco walls. It wasn't quite a warehouse, it looked like it was in the process of being built still.

I tried to think of any large buildings being built near the small Mesa airport. I passed the area on the highway often when I used the 202 to get to Akira's place quickly. There were a few but if Fa'gh was being truthful, and I'm pretty sure he was because why lie to someone you're going to watch die soon, it was a large building being put up next to a counter and cabinet store right off of the Power Road exit. Now I just needed to find a way to tell Lucien.

Siobal. Ghosts. I could see if I could call Siobal to me. She couldn't communicate with anyone alive but she had mentioned talking to Spirit around Shane. Maybe that could work, if Spirit was willing to help me again. It was worth a shot.

Taking a deep breath, I closed my eyes and emptied my mind of my pain, of the loss of Akira, and tried to call Siobal. I did as she always told me to do, I focused on what I wanted and on just that. I'm not sure how long I focused on calling her but when I opened my eyes, the sun had started to set and it was dark within the warehouse and Siobal was sitting in front of me with her face twisted in worry. I glanced down and my skin glowed but I hoped Fa'gh was too preoccupied to notice.

What felt like hope blossomed from the overwhelming bleakness I had been feeling right after I remembered Akira being killed. I looked at Fa'gh who might have been sleeping but I couldn't tell. Siobal shook her head at me.

"He's not asleep. He's just mediating. He's waiting for the man who contracted him to arrive. Don't say anything. Just nod that you understand." I nod and she continues. "I thought that if you were still alive, you'd call for me when you could. I spoke with Spirit and she is going to relay anything I can find out here to Shane."

That was exactly what I had wanted to happen. Siobal was already a few steps ahead of me. I nodded at her, trying not to draw Fa'gh's attention.

"I think I know where we are but I'll be able to tell when I look outside. I'll go tell Spirit as fast as I can but you need to hang in there. The MEPA and the wolf pack are scouring the valley. I believe they are near this location but it will take time to get them here. That demon," she spat out angrily, "is using some kind of cloaking magic that isn't letting them track you by scent or magic. There's a unit nearby but Shane isn't with them." She placed her hand on my cheek and I felt the cool touch in this unending heat. "Just try to stay alive, ok?" She disappeared shortly after. I focused on my breathing and willed my skin to stop glowing.

The hope dulled slightly but I wouldn't let it be overcome with that bleakness again. Akira would want me to fight back. He would kick my butt if I gave up and let this demon win. We were going to catch the man who had brought this demon back and punish him. I knew Shax would get rid of Fa'gh with his dagger.

Shrugging my shoulders, I tested to see how tight the rope was around me. That's what the people did in the movies, right? All it did was cause the pain in my right side to flare and I bit my lip to stop the cry that threatened to come out. This was not going to be easy.

Before I could try something else, the door on the far end of the warehouse opened and someone stepped through before closing it quickly. I couldn't see who it was, it was starting to become too dark and there was only one light on above us. Electricity conscious evil demon, who knew?

Squinting I watched as the figure got closer and my eyes widened as recognition made me gasp. The man who walked with a strut toward the demon and held the Staff of Malum, wasn't a man at all. It was a gnome. It was Carl.

"What in the actual fuck? Carl?!"

How was this possible? Gnome's didn't necessarily have a lot of magic and the magic they did have tended to be put toward electronics. You didn't think that Steve Jobs didn't have some kind of magical help, did you?

Carl's face grimaced in a malicious twist. His upper lip curled and he spit at his feet. His skin was off color, like he hadn't gotten much sleep lately. (Contracting with a demon could cause that, big surprise there). He looked sick compared to when I saw him outside of his glamor near the grocery store the other day.

"You finally got her." Carl basically hissed at Fa'gh. "You were supposed to capture her days ago!"

"She was protected by a powerful wizard and those damn werewolves kept sniffing around where they weren't wanted. She's here now. Our contract is complete once you've killed her. Hurry up."

"Wait!" I glanced between them. "Why are you doing this, Carl? How did you even manage to contract with a demon?"

That's when Carl smirked and the strut, he thought was sexy, came back into his step as he came to squat in front of me. A light glinted off something around his neck and my eyes narrowed in on it. Siobal's power crystal. What was he doing with it?

"Why am I doing this?" He gripped my hair in his hand and yanked my face up. It didn't hurt all that much but it was annoying. "When I found the staff, it was covered in grime and forgotten under boxes in an old magical storage unit that I was cleaning out." He yanked my hair again and let go. "Fa'gh was all too willing to help me get revenge on those who had belittled me. If he brought the people I hated to me and helped me kill them, I would give him what magic I have so that he could be free of the staff's influence to walk the Earth once again."

He stood up from his crouch and walked back a few steps and started pacing. "But it's taken longer than I wanted it too. You're the last on my list of people I want killed. You always cut off my drinks before everyone else or you never let me drink in the first place! You're the worst of them from the bar. You always looked down at me like you were better than I am! You're practically human and you have the audacity to tell me I can't drink when I want to?"

Well, that settled that. Carl was insane with a few nuts and bolts loose when his mother drop kicked him on his head as a baby.

"You killed people because they basically annoyed you? What in the hell is wrong with you? You are seriously demented. I cut you off when you were too drunk to stand so that you wouldn't hurt yourself or someone else. I didn't let you put anything on a tab because the one time we did that without a credit card you didn't pay for two months." My voice steadily rose until I was shouting up at the short gnome. "You're fucking insane, you three-foot-tall shithead!"

Carl hissed at me; his grey teeth flashed as if he wanted to tear into my throat. "You dare make fun of me, even now that you're about to be killed?" His right foot kicked me in the stomach and that hurt because it made me jerk and my right side felt like it was on fire. "I am going to have so much fun carving up your face. Fa'gh is going to eat your eyeballs!"

I curled up as tightly as I could and mustered a halfhearted laugh. An idea on how to stall them came to me as he had been ranting.

"I can't believe that Fa'gh fell for the shit you have spewing out of your mouth. I have more magic than you do. You have barely enough magic to glamour around humans." I taunted at Carl but watched Fa'gh. The demon had straightened out as I spoke and his eyes had flared as he looked at Carl.

"What is she talking about? You have magic. You are able to activate the staff and summon me forth to make the contract."

Carl began to look nervous but he turned his back on me to face Fa'gh. The idiot.

"Of course, I have magic!" He had started to sweat and I was certain it wasn't anything to do with the temperature. "Like you said. I activated the staff. She's just trying to piss us off."

"He's not wrong. I do want to piss you off. You kidnapped me and killed the love of my life." I spit at both of them. "But I'm also telling the truth. Everyone knows that Carl has barely any magic. He's not allowed to work in the tech field with his fellow gnomes, he had to get a job as a cleaner for a magical waste company. He probably used most of his magic to activate the staff." Now I was just shooting in the dark hoping that it somehow made sense to Fa'gh and didn't sound like I had no idea what I was talking about, which in part, I didn't.

Carl backed up toward the door holding the staff in front of him. "Now, that's not true! I have enough magic to give you that'll let you get free from the staff. Just let me kill her so our contract is complete. Everyone knows that a demon has to abide by the contracts they make or be thrust back into hell."

Fa'gh had started to slowly walk toward Carl and was emitting a low and terrible growl that sent shudders down my spine. I wanted to run. Maybe this hadn't been such a good idea. What happened if Fa'gh killed Carl? He wouldn't have any reason to keep me alive. Crudbuckets. I probably should have thought this through more.

"Wait!" I try to distract Fa'gh. "Why do you even want to separate from the staff? There're no free demons on Earth anymore. You'll just be hunted down and killed."

He paused in his stalking of Carl to look back at me. "It's cute how the supernatural and humans think demons have all but disappeared. We just hide better. Not to mention with how violent humans have become, it makes it all the much easier to hide in plain sight."

It was just a day for unfortunate news. Demons roaming free on

Earth was a powder keg just waiting to blow. Where was Lucien? I was in way over my head.

"She's just trying to make it so I don't kill her. She's trying to get us to turn on each other." Carl's gravelly voice interrupted my thoughts. "Let me kill her and I'll fulfill my end of the contract."

Fa'gh was still looking at me but he was flicking his fingers in irritation. I had a small hope that he'd turn back and deal with Carl but luck was not on my side. He nodded at Carl.

"Hear me, gnome. After you have your revenge, you WILL surrender your magic to me so that I may finally be free."

Carl was looking even more sick than he had when he had first entered the warehouse but he nodded in agreement. "As agreed."

He pulled out a small but deadly looking knife from within his shirt and I vaguely wondered how he didn't cut himself. It wasn't the best time to think about things like that since he was back to his plan of killing me. I glared up at Carl. Fuck it. If this gnome was going to kill me, I would make sure to come back and haunt him.

Carl held his knife above his head as he stood in front of me and I saw his muscles bunch as he readied himself to stab me but there was suddenly a loud boom from the outside and the metal door shook. Carl took a step back as he looked toward the door.

"This is the MEPA! Come out with your hands in the air." A voice cut through the warehouse and I almost cried out. That voice belonged to Shane. Siobal had done it.

While Carl cursed and turned to Fa'gh, they started arguing, I figured it would be smart to try to get some distance between myself and them. Even if I had to roll.

Which is what I ended up doing as quietly as I could but when I rolled and my right side hit the concrete floor, I had to bite my inner cheek to stop from crying out in pain.

"What do we do now? There's not a lot of options on getting out of here." Carl had started to pace.

Fa'gh seemed surprisingly calm about the situation. "Let them come. They can't kill me."

Carl hissed at him, spittle flying. "But they can kill me and then who will help you?"

Fa'gh shrugged at Carl as if he hadn't a care in the world. "Fine. Give me your magic now and I will get rid of them."

I had managed to roll about halfway toward the metal door without being noticed but it was only going to be a matter of time before they figured it out. There was another large boom.

"This is your last warning." Shane's tone was no nonsense and Carl was ready to bolt.

"Fine! I'll give you my magic, free and clear. How do I do this?" He was basically vibrating where he stood. I was watching Fa'gh as I took a second to breathe through the pain, a chill went down my spine as he watched Carl with a sneer.

"That's all that was needed. Your acknowledgment that you give your magic to me." His tone was gleeful and I started scooting backward toward the door again, whatever he was about to do would not end well.

"I don't feel any different." Carl looked at his hands.

"Oh, you will." Fa'ghs right hand pierced through Carl's stomach until his claws could be seen on the other side. He lifted Carl up like he was a stuffed animal and his piranha teeth gleamed against the light. "It has not been a pleasure working with you." As he opened his mouth, he pulled Carl closer and there was a faint, at first, yellow light that started to glow from Carl's mouth. Fa'gh took a deep breath in and as he did, that glow around Carl started to flow into Fa'gh's mouth. Talk about fast food for demons...

Carl's mouth gaped open and a thin line of blood leaked from its side as he slowly lost color in his face as Fa'gh continued to suck the glowing yellow light from Carl. I was assuming that glow was Carl's magic. Now if he had to die to give it up, that's a question I would not be asking the demon. I tried to find sympathy for the gnome but he didn't deserve it. Not after all he had done.

There was another large boom and heat rushed in, searing my back as a gust of wind blew in the doors. I managed to look behind me and I could have cried at the sight. The first thing I saw was Lucien and Shax running decked out in MEPA protective gear and helmets. There were several MEPA agents behind them and a few of Uncle Ray's wolves.

Lucien's eyes met mine and I could see relief flood his face. There was a thump in front of me and as I looked back over, Carl had been dropped on the ground and Fa'gh wiped his mouth with his arm.

"That was the best taste so far. You were right, though." He looked at me and seemed unconcerned about the havoc that was happening in front of him. I could hear the MEPA agents running in and commands that were being given behind me as if they were miles away. "He barely had any magic but it's enough to do what I need."

There was a hand on my shoulder that had metal fingers that filled my heart with warmth. Lucien's voice whispered in my ear. "Hold on, sweetie. I'm getting the ropes off of you and I'll get you out of here."

Shax walked past us and stood in front of Fa'gh who had picked up the staff.

"Well, well. If it isn't Fa'gh the parasite demon." I couldn't see Shax's face but Fa'gh looked angry, like someone had pissed in his cheerios. "My father sends his regards." Shax voice had taken on an other-worldly tone that almost echoed. He pulled out his black dagger and twisted it so that the light caught on it.

Lucien tugged gently on my shoulder and I jerked to attention, I had been so focused on Shax that I had forgotten that I had been tied up. Lucien pulled me up to a sitting position and he cupped my face in his hands. "It's going to be okay now but we need to get out of here. Are you able to walk?" I took stock of my body and nodded. I was in pain but not enough that I couldn't stand on my own. Any physical pain I felt was nothing compared to the anguish I was blocking from Akira's death.

Lucien helped me stand as Shax continued to distract the demon who was becoming increasingly malevolent and watched, fascinated, as the staff started to flash a bright red within Fa'gh's grip. The demon seemed to be growing larger in size as we watched. Shax still looked bored and he shifted slightly, his body relaxed but I knew him, he was ready to spring at the right moment.

Lucien had taken my hand and was moving slowly backward, toward the rest of the MEPA agents. We stepped as quietly and slowly as we could so that we didn't draw attention from Fa'gh. What was only a few minutes felt like hours as we moved.

"Growing in size is not going to make the females want you, no matter how big you think you need to be." Shax was taunting Fa'gh now. "You have to know that just the sight of you makes anyone want to stab their eyes out." The wolves had spread out around Fa'gh while Shax taunted him.

"Your childish taunts mean nothing to me, child spawn. You are just a speck. Your mother should have smothered you as soon as you left her womb." Fa'gh was now easily twice as tall and wide as Shax who stood in front of him, it was like he was draining the staff's power.

We had made it to the doors of the warehouse and Lucien pushed me toward Shane.

"Stay with Shane. The healers will be with you soon!" He moved off toward Shax before I could say anything.

I stepped to follow him on instinct but Shane placed his hand on my shoulder, pulling me back. When I looked up at him, the smile that usually was on his face was replaced with a grim frown.

"Let them do their job, child." His voice had turned grave as he glanced toward where Lucien approached Fa'gh.

I hated that I felt so useless but there wasn't anything I could do to help; I would just get in the way and that might get someone else killed. I clenched my hands together as I watched my ex-boyfriend and current lover face off against a monster.

CHAPTER 14

F a'gh seemed to stop growing finally and the staff had stopped flashing. It was with the power he stole from Carl that he was able to steal the staff's power and that was a terrifying thought. I looked up at Shane and shared my thoughts.

"That's what looks like has happened." Shane shook his head. "It shouldn't be possible. With the research I found on The Staff of Malum, it should only be able to enhance magic, yes, but what it looks like he's done, like you noticed, he's taken the magic of the staff into himself. Just like a power crystal, the staff is used to store and enhance magic users. I can only imagine the kind of power that Fa'gh now has."

He turned toward the agents that were barricaded behind a large ward that had been set up. "Spread out. I need a three mile ward to hide whatever happens here from the humans. We'll need the ward to cover the sky above the warehouse as well. There's no telling what is going to happen and how far this fight is going to go."

The agents broke off into teams, some ran to vehicles that were idling nearby. I watched as a pair of agents started drawing the start of several wards moving opposite of each other and the magic was almost visible in the air as other agents started their own. I jumped slightly when Siobal popped up out of nowhere next to me.

"You're alright." She frowned as she looked at Fa'gh. "This is getting bad. I don't think they are going to be able to defeat him if they don't work together."

"What do you mean?" I glanced at Lucien and noticed he and the agents who had gone into the warehouse with him were working in sync. "They look like they've done this before."

"They most likely have worked together before. But your ex? He's never worked with them and he's most likely used to dealing with things on his own. He has the only way of killing Fa'gh permanently. And the werewolves are just getting in the way."

Before I could think of something to say, Fa'gh struck. He was casually avoiding the lunges from the werewolves as if it was a game one second and the next, he was on top of one of the MEPA agents, his claws disemboweling the poor man before anyone could react. His screams were cut short as Fa'gh twisted the man's head almost all the way off. Gasping in horror, no one could look away.

Lucien yelled a command and the remaining agents formed a circle together, chanting softly as a spell began to build. Lucien stood in front of them and yelled at Fa'gh.

"Why don't you attack someone who isn't afraid of you?" He held a stance of a martial artist, the hand with his metal prosthetics was palm up and straight out, the other a fist near his waist as he bent his knees. Electricity appeared along his limbs, his magic building in response to his command.

Fa'gh's answer was a deep laugh that would make any sane person run in the opposite direction. Lucien, clearly, was not a sane man. The hand that was palm up curved inward and Lucien yelled out a word that activated his lightning spell and it flew straight at Fa'gh. It was almost blinding, the lightning that streaked across the room but just as it was about to hit Fa'gh, the demon wasn't there again. Lucien cursed and looked around, as did his agents.

"I'm getting bored with you, demon." Shax spoke from where he was last, not having moved from the spot. I narrowed my eyes as I looked at his face as he turned toward the door. His bright green eyes met mine and he smirked at me, a hint of fangs that I had never seen before appearing. Since when did he have fangs?

"What the...?" I mumbled out loud.

"What is it, lass?" Shane was still at my side.

"Shax," I tried to describe the feeling of unease that suddenly flared within, "there's something different."

There was another scream, this one filled with rage, as Fa'gh dropped from above Shax toward him. He must have jumped there after Lucien's attack. A scream froze in my throat to warn Shax but I didn't need to worry.

In an astounding show of lithe agility, Shax rolled away from the attack and came out of the roll with the dagger in his hand. He jumped toward Fa'gh and managed to slice across the demons left calf as he attempted to get away from Shax. His roar of pain was satisfying to listen to. I wasn't the only one who thought so, either. Several agents around us cheered as Shax literally seemed to be dancing away from Fa'gh's attempts to slice him to ribbons with his claws.

Not to be forgotten, Lucien shouted at Shax to duck as he tumbled away from a swipe from Fa'gh's claws that got too close for comfort. Shax either didn't hear him or had decided to ignore him because instead of ducking he had thrust the dagger in an arc toward Fa'gh and cursed as the demon managed to knock his arm aside. The dagger went flying across the floor and out of sight into the darker part of the warehouse. Fa'gh prevented him from going after the dagger.

"That's what I was worried about." Siobals soft voice carried over the fighting. "They need to work together."

Even without the dagger, Shax didn't give up. He used his body, and to my surprise, earth and ice magic, to fight back against the parasite demon. He was almost a blur as he dodged the claws that were trying to kill him and ice erupted from his hands. He would throw ice at Fa'gh, and it would hurt him, but the demon healed almost instantly. The only wound that hadn't healed was on his left calf from the dagger.

One wolf jumped on top of Fa'gh from behind, burying its teeth into the demon's shoulder as the other two rounded to the front of the demon, jumping on his chest. Each wolf probably weighed close to three hundred pounds but Fa'gh didn't even blink. He roared as he grabbed the wolf on his back and threw him across the room while batting at the two who kept trying to jump on his chest. Shax had to dive out of the way when the wolf who was thrown almost rammed into him.

"Shane," I looked up at him, "Siobal made a point that Lucien and Shax and the wolves need to work together. And we need to find that dagger." I gestured to the fight as Lucien and his agents joined in the fight again with lightning spells that almost hit Shax but missed Fa'gh as the large demon seemed to be able to sense where the next hit was coming from. "Can you get their attention? I hate to say it, but my uncle's wolves probably need to get out of the way."

Shane touched a small device near his left shoulder. "I can. We find that electronic communication in these situations works better than magic." He clicked a button and spoke into the device. It was a shoulder mic. "Lucien. Stop throwing magic haphazardly and work with Shax to contain this demon. Right now, he's making you look like idiots. Shax, start paying attention to your surroundings. You're not the only one in there." Shane barked into the mic. I thought Lucien was in charge but maybe he wasn't. "Wolves," This time he glanced at a wolf who appeared on the other side of the car where we stood. I recognized his black markings across his muzzle, it was Sean, "I need you to pull out and let my men do their jobs."

I didn't wait to see Sean's reaction and I turned toward Siobal. "Siobal, can I ask you for one more favor? Can you find the dagger and show me where it is?"

"I like the way you think." Siobal flew off into the warehouse and I turned toward Shane as Rick threw his head back and howled, signaling the wolves inside to retreat.

"They need to focus on fighting Fa'gh together. Keep him distracted enough that he doesn't realize I'm in there again getting the dagger for Shax." I made sure my chin was tipped up and tried to act like I knew what I was doing. In reality, I was shaking in fear but I was the only one Siobal could interact with beside Spirit and Shane was busy supervising the MEPA agents. "I've got to help them."

Shane stared down at me but it took a few seconds before he spoke. "Alright, ghost girl, I'll work on those idiots and make them work together to distract the demon while you get that dagger. Don't die." With that he went back to watching the fight and yelling instructions into the mic.

The wolves ran past us, one on three legs as it dragged its fourth. Sean turned his head toward me and I walked to him and touched his head. "It's going to be ok. Trust me." He bowed his head and ran off to the other wolves. It was good to be the alpha's niece sometimes.

Breathing in and holding it, I counted backward from ten to try to calm down, while I focused on the fight and waited for Siobal to return. The sun had set and now the only light inside of the warehouse was that single one on the ceiling and the flood lights from the MEPA agents' cars.

Lucien now stood back to back with Shax. Fa'gh had disappeared again but that didn't last long because he jumped from the side trying to take out both of them with his claws when they turned together and shot a combination of ice and lightning into his chest. Fa'gh kept their attention and there was no way that they would be able to look for the dagger and fight him at the same time. Not without one of them getting hurt or killed. There was a harsh smell of burned skin that was wafting out of the warehouse and I tried not to gag.

Lucien didn't stop at just throwing lightning. He ran toward Fa'gh who was on his hands and knees after the last attack. He pulled up his hand as he ran at him and sliced downward in an arc. What could only be described as a long lightning sword cut through the air and into Fa'gh. The demon roared as his right arm slid to the ground in a loud plopping noise and blood spurted from his shoulder. He would be able to grow his arm back but that looked like it would slow the parasite down, at least enough time to do more damage. Shax was right behind Lucien as he ran at the demon. Ice surrounded his fist as he slammed it into Fa'gh's chin, jerking his head up and he rolled out of the way of the two fighters. The other MEPA agents seemed to be building a containment circle on the ground and were steadily ignoring the fight behind them.

That's when Siobal came flying out of the warehouse door. "I found it. It's on the far right side of the warehouse. It got stuck in-between the wall and some discarded wood." She gestured to me and I ran toward her. "Let's get that dagger and end this."

Running toward the danger and not away from it was probably a stupid idea. My mother would call me an idiot and tell me that being a hero served no purpose in this day and age. But I wasn't trying to be a hero, I just wanted this to end. That thought spurred me on as I had to dive to the right as soon as I went through the warehouse door as a large group of ice shards sailed through the air and out toward where Shane and the other agents were.

"Sorry!" Shax barely looked back as he had to throw himself backward to avoid Fa'gh's remaining arm as it slashed out at him.

My eyes tried to adjust to the darkness but with the flashes of lightning, my visibility went from almost daylight to midnight rapidly. Siobal hovered at my side as she told me where to go. I tried to keep myself small and ran along the wall toward the far side of the warehouse where Siobal said the dagger was. It wasn't that easy as I had to stop several times as my right side flared with so much pain. I was starting to see dark circles in my vision.

As I got further from the fight, the darker it became. This was a much larger warehouse than I thought it was at first... Perhaps it just seemed larger because I was trying to find a dagger in the darkness that would help kill a demon. There was that.

About halfway toward the area Siobal was leading me to I stumbled over something in the dark and I fell to my hands. I winced as my knees hit the hard concrete floor and looked to what I had tripped over.

Carl's dead body and blank eyes stared back at me and I scrambled backward with a yip and ignored the flash of pain again. I gulped air greedily as I shook my head. He was dead now and couldn't hurt anyone else again.

"Hurry!" Siobal hissed at me. "The demon's arm is starting to regrow and I don't think your guys are going to hold out much longer. They're tiring out."

"Right." I stood carefully but before I turned around again, I remembered that Carl had Siobal's power crystal around his neck. I leaned over and saw that it was still there. Chanting "ewewew" I pulled the necklace off of Carl's dead body and put it around my neck. I turned back to follow Siobal.

I refused to look over at the fight as a burst of speed ran through me and I was soon at the area Siobal said the dagger was. At first, I didn't see it. It was hidden underneath a pile of scrap wood like she had mentioned but it was stuck. I grabbed the hilt and pulled but it didn't move. I grasped the hilt this time with both hands and braced my legs apart and pulled as hard as I could. Pain stabbed my right side and this time I had blacked out for a few seconds.

When I opened my eyes again, I was flat on my back and it was hard to breath. Siobal was hovering over me, her eyes concerned. A groan slipped out as I pushed myself into a sitting position and clutched my right side. I think I broke a few ribs but couldn't be sure.

The dagger was on the ground next to me and I grabbed it, ignoring the pain in my right side as I got to my feet. There would be time later to cry about my pain, emotionally and physically, but right now, my men needed this dagger.

The situation had changed in the fight between the time I had passed out and now. Fa'gh was in the middle of the containment spell that the other agents on Lucien's team had built. It was a circle ward and light flared upward toward the ceiling, crisscrossing and flared brightly when Fa'gh threw himself at the edge of the circle. It bounced him backwards as he kept slamming into it over and over again. But every time he hit the walls; the light would lessen. His right arm was almost halfway regrown, it was a stump and the flesh looked like it was rotting off as it grew.

Lucien stood with his legs braced and hands up against the warded circle and was enforcing the spell but he looked exhausted. His magic was draining, even a wizard has his limits. Shax was on the other side of the warehouse, looking for the dagger.

"Shax!" I had to scream his name. "Over here!" I waved the dagger in the air to get his attention.

Shax turned toward my voice and his face broke out in a grin and he ran toward me. He wasn't the only one who heard me though. Fa'gh looked my way and his face was turned into a snarl as he locked eyes on the dagger.

"Stupid human!" He roared and slammed against the ward and the magic flared but the light started to crack like glass. Fa'gh noticed and his snarls turned into laughter as he rammed into the ward again.

Shax was almost to me when the parasite demon broke through the ward. The magic flashed and the agents and Lucien were thrown backward to find themselves slammed hard into the concrete ground. I screamed Lucien's name but he didn't move. Shax turned toward Fa'gh and ice shards formed in a circle around him.

"Sorry, baby. I'll distract the big lug here. Think you can get that dagger into his side?" He flashed a cocky grin back at me. "I'm almost out of gas. Without him in the containment spell, there's no way I can focus on stabbing him and holding him off of you and the others." He threw his hands down into the ground with ice wrapping around his arms. As his hands met the ground, a crack started to form rapidly moving toward Fa'gh who was running full out toward us. The crack split into two as it rushed forward. He was using both his ice and earth magic.

My hands shook but I clutched the dagger hilt to my chest. He wanted me to stab Fa'gh with it. Sure. That sounded easy enough.

Stab a rampaging demon hellbent on killing everyone to get to his freedom. It sounded doable. Totally doable, right?

The crack that formed when Shax hit the ground with his hands continued to grow and what looked like lava, started bubbling out. The crack ran toward Fa'gh and formed a circle around him, which caused the demon to stop suddenly and he backed away from the bubbling lava that seemed to grow higher with each passing second. That was something I hadn't expected.

"You." His gravel voice shouted into the dark. "How can you control ice and earth? You are nothing but a spawn who should have died in your mother's womb."

A self-deprecating chuckle came from Shax as he pushed his hands deeper into the crack and more lava spewed. The demon did not want the stuff touching him.

"Well," his eyes flashed in pain, "even if that were true, I still have more magic than a parasite demon." The lava started to ooze out more slowly, the concrete seeming to melt in on itself as it spread in a circle around Fa'gh who attempted to avoid any spews from it.

"Vic," Shax muttered to me, "I'm going to pull him to me using the lava. Be ready and don't hesitate. Stab him in the side on the heart side or in the back near the heart. He's lost enough magic he stole that it should slow him enough to allow me to finish it." He glanced at me, and even though his face was pale, his lips looked almost non-existent with how white they were, he managed to give me his playful smirk. "Let's end this."

I pulled my shoulders back and focused on the situation. I emptied my mind and focused on the only thing that mattered at this moment. Stabbing Fa'gh without getting killed. I emptied my thoughts of everything but the focused goal. The pain slipped away as the world narrowed around the three of us. I looked to the dagger and my hand glowed with my internal power supporting me.

I moved off from Shax's side to his right, if I was going to aim for as close to Fa'gh's heart as I could, I needed to be on the right side. I didn't go far but I focused on being just far enough that Fa'gh wouldn't see me coming from behind. I tried to stay as small as possible by bending but keeping myself ready to sprint when it was time. As long as Shax kept his attention, he wouldn't know I was there until the dagger was already in him.

"Why don't you just give yourself up?" Shax was taunting Fa'agh. "My hellfire can just as easily make you wish that you were dead. You remember its hold on you when you lived there?" The cracks in the concrete widened again as lava, or what he referred to as hellfire, circled around Fa'gh where there was only one way for him to go to avoid it. He had to move forward toward Shax.

The parasite demon didn't like that he was cornered and, in his rage, he threw his head back and roared, his teeth flashing as he ran toward Shax, just barely avoiding the cracks that appeared around him. The demon's left arm reached up as he got ready to slash at Shax who was vulnerable at this point with his hands sunken into the ground. He was that way because he trusted me and I wasn't going to let him down. I couldn't, not after I let Akira down.

I waited and just as Fa'gh passed me, stopped just short of Shax and started to swing his left arm downward to strike at Shax, I was already sprinting toward him. This was it. I had to stab him or he was going to kill Shax and take another person I cared about away. Drawing on that calming power that was mine now, I focused and saw where I would strike clearly.

When he grew, he had easily topped seven feet and had widened, and in this case, it was in my favor. I was only able to reach his side but I aimed at just under his armpit where there would be less chance to hit ribs. He forgot about me and that was his mistake. Shax's lava moved around me as I ran at the parasite demon.

Gripping the dagger hilt in both hands, I threw my weight into my thrust and the dagger sank into his muscles. It wasn't easy, not like how television shows it. Stabbing through muscle is hard but the dagger seemed to come alive almost as if Fa'gh's blood fed it and pushed in deeper.

Fa'gh let out a strangled scream of pain that sounded like the roar

of a wounded animal. I pulled the dagger out of him and moved backward as quickly as I could. Fa'gh turned toward me, his left arm strug-
gling to lift as blood gushed from the wound that I had given him. His
right arm had just started to form his hand and he started to step after
me but Shax's lava was there in his way, now closed into a full circle.

Shax stood from where he knelt, but he wobbled as he straightened. Sweat was pouring down his face and his shirt was soaked. His
eyes met mine and I could almost see the smile that he was holding
back as he made his way over to me. I held up the dagger for him,
making sure it was pointed down and the hilt up for him to grab.
When he took it, his hand engulfed mine and squeezed.

"You were fearless, V." He whispered softly. "Great job. Now, let
me finish this idiot and we're going to celebrate later, alright?" He
winked in his usual flirty fashion and faced Fa'gh who was beginning
to look worse with every passing minute.

Where the stab wound was, the flesh seemed to be disintegrating
around the wound, his blood that continued to flow out of the wound
was black and the area of blackened skin grew. He was pacing within
the circle of fire but he was getting slower as he did.

"It's over, Fa'gh." Shax approached the fire circle nonchalantly as
if he were on a morning walk. "You know it. I know it. She knows it.
That wound is going to slowly take your life essence away and you're
going to be in agonizing pain the whole time. You can feel it, right?"
He stopped just short of the circle of spewing lava. If he reached out
his arm would go through the lava to within the circle.

"Stupid, spawn." Fa'gh gasped each word. "I hope you burn in
Hell with the others for all of time." He fell to his knees. "Just wait
until that girl finds out what you really are." He coughed and choked
on a laugh. "She'll go running for the hills the second she realizes she
was bedded by the likes of you." He threw his head back and through
his coughing he laughed even as blackened blood choked out.

Shax stepped through the lava swiftly as it parted for him and
stood in front of Fa'gh. "May you suffer eternally." His voice was
formal and he slammed the dagger into Fa'gh's chest and pierced the

heart as he twisted the knife. Fa'gh's choking laughter slowly died as he slumped backwards as Shax removed the dagger from his chest. The demons body hit the concrete with a solid thud and Shax stepped through the fire circle unharmed. He knelt on one knee and pressed his left hand into the ground again like he did before and Fa'gh's body was engulfed by lava and flames.

Shax glanced up at me. "Why don't we go see the detective and the MEPA agents? Make sure everyone is okay? My hellfire will finish destroying his body." He stood and wiped the dagger clean using the corner of his shirt. I felt a little bit of bile rise.

CHAPTER 15

I was lying in a small hospital bed located in the medical ward at the MEPA headquarters in Phoenix a few days after. After Shax finished off Fa'gh we were swarmed by agents and healer personnel. Lucien had cracked his head open when he and the other agents had been hit with the backlash of their own containment spell. He had to have the healers work on him for a couple of hours to heal the internal injuries. Shax was deemed fit but magically exhausted and ordered on bed rest for a few days.

I, on the other hand, ended up with several broken ribs and a punctured lung. The healers were surprised I stayed conscious as long as I had and that I had been able to walk, much less run. The healers were able to work their magic on me, but boy, did it come with a heavy price of additional pain. They placed me under a sleeping spell and took me to their medical ward.

Shax was located in a different room, they wouldn't move him to mine, no matter how hard he argued. I could hear him grumbling from my room when they woke me up almost six days later. My cell phone had been destroyed sometime during the fight or before so I didn't have any way to communicate with anyone outside of the medical ward since they didn't have any phones in the rooms. The supervisor who had woken me up said they had called my family and Lucien to let them know I was awake.

And Akira. Akira was gone. It felt like my heart was no longer beating and there was just this weight in my chest. I couldn't even cry it hurt so much to think about him being gone.

My mind kept going to memories growing up with him in my life. The first day that I had seen him when he came to the bar to meet with Uncle Ray to ask to be part of the pack. He had shorter hair back then with no red tips, but his silver eyes instantly pierced through my heart and I fell for him within that heartbeat. The memory of him punching Shax in my defense. All the nights we spent playing Xbox and where he mostly kicked my ass at the games. Our first kiss against the wall outside of the bar. Watching him make out with Lucien for the first time. Everything was just memories now and I wouldn't get the chance to make more.

It was later in the day after I was woken from the sleeping spell when a healer brought in some clothes for me and let me know that I had visitors. I nodded as I took the clothes from him and started to dress.

I paused momentarily as I saw Siobal's power crystal on top of the pile. I picked it up gingerly and ran my fingers along the length. It was a beautiful white and my fingers tingled as they ran along it. I hugged the necklace to my chest and looked up to Siobal who stood looking out the window.

"You did it." She seemed sad. "You stopped him and avenged my death." When she turned toward me, she was crying. I hadn't known that a ghost could cry until that moment.

"Thank you." She walked to stand in front of me and closed her hand over mine that held the crystal. "This is yours now. You have so much power within you that's been just waiting to be released. And it's not just going to be vision related, I think you have a real gift with your ghost magic. I may have given you some of my power, the ability to see visions, but it's your own that made them that accurate. It took me hours of sex to build up what you were able to do in a ward circle."

I clenched the crystal tighter and swallowed. "Thank you, Siobal. For everything."

"You never know." Her eyes sparkled. "I might just be back to visit." She leaned forward and pressed her lips to my right cheek. It was a cool touch but it filled me with warmth. "Until then, I'll see you." And just like that she was gone. I pulled the necklace on as I stood to get dressed.

I had just pulled on my jeans with only a slight ache in my right side when there was a knock on the door. I looked up as Uncle Ray walked in carrying a bundle of balloons and flowers that blocked the doorway. I laughed as he cursed and fumbled to get it through the doorway.

"Uncle Ray!" I waited at the bed for him to get through. "I'm so glad to see you."

"Hey, Vic!" Uncle's Ray's voice was muffled as he finally got through the door with all the balloons and flowers. "We brought some food, too. Figured the food here might be just as bad as human hospital food."

Behind Uncle Ray came Chase, Sean, and Lucien. I ran at Lucien, ignoring everyone else who was still filtering through the room. My heart felt like it was in my throat as Lucien came to my side and enveloped me in his arms. I breathed in his scent and relaxed and went almost limp in his arms.

"Vic," Lucien kissed my forehead, "You are amazing and I am so glad you're ok."

"Lucien," my voice was already trembling, "Akira...he..."

"I, what?" That familiar Texan drawl came behind Lucien's back at the doorway.

I froze in Lucien's arms and dug my nails into his chest. He couldn't be. I couldn't see him as a ghost. That was even more cruel than him being dead. I buried my face into Lucien's shirt.

"What did I do, V?" Akira's voice sounded concerned now and closer, right next to us.

"No, no, no, no." I shook my head, slamming my eyes shut and clamped my hands over my ears.

"Vickie, what's the matter?" Lucien pulled me back from his arms and I felt him tip my chin up.

"What did you do to my niece, Akira?" Uncle Ray's voice boomed through the room.

"I didn't do anything!" Akira argued back and there was an edge of concern in his voice.

Wait. If he were a ghost, Uncle Ray wouldn't be able to talk to him. I opened my eyes and my arms lowered as I looked over to where Akira's voice came from.

There he stood. In his too tight jeans and adorable plaid button up shirt. His hair was ruffled, it looked like he hadn't shaved for a few days and his eyes were furrowed in concern.

He was alive?

I stepped away from Lucien's arms and toward Akira.

"You're alive?" I whispered as my fingers reached up to brush against his scruffy chin. "You didn't die? I saw you die. Fa'gh stabbed you through the heart and your eyes were blank!" My voice was steadily rising as I spoke and came close to shouting by the end.

"Oh, my love." Akira swept me up into his arms, lifting my feet off the ground as he hugged me close. "No, I didn't die. Our Bubble Butt here was only a few minutes away and his healers were able to heal my shredded heart enough for my body to heal itself. Oh sweetie. I didn't know that you thought I was dead." He buried his face in my neck as I started to sob into his shoulder. My heart that had felt so broken started to knit itself back together.

"I think we should give them some space. We'll come back in an hour or so." Uncle Ray's command swept through the room and soon I heard the door close shut behind them after what sounded like a brief scuffle.

I looked up and saw that everyone had left the room, including

Lucien. I hadn't wanted him to go and a whimper left my mouth before I could stop it. I needed both of them near me right now. Akira seemed to feel the same because he went to the door, still holding me up, yanked it open. Lucien wasn't anywhere to be seen. Lucien had to want to be with us too, right?

"Akira, go find our Bubble Butt." I wiped the tears from my face. He could get him back quicker than I could and I wanted to speak to Shax now that I was allowed out of bed. "I'm going to go to Shax's room and thank him."

Akira huffed but agreed without comment as he placed me back onto the ground and tilted his head up, his nostrils flaring as he sought out Lucien's scent. He went off toward the left and around the corner. I smiled, clutching my chest in relief. Shaking my head slightly I asked one of the apprentice healers that was passing me where Shax was. It turned out he was only three rooms down from mine.

I knocked on his open door as I stepped in. He was laying spread out on the bed with his arms behind his head. He looked better from the last time I had seen him. At the end of the fight, he had looked close to Death's door. Now, his color was back and his eyes were sparking with his normal mischievous self.

"Hey, there she is. The hero of the hour!" He sat up, swinging his legs over the bedside as I approached and patted the side next to him.

I snorted then sat next to him and glanced up into his face. "I'm not a hero. You're the one who almost drained your magic dry to kill him. I'm glad you're alright. I wanted to say thank you. You didn't have to come back and help but you did."

Shax looked at the floor, his right leg bouncing up and down. "Can I be honest with you?" He sounded wary.

"That would be good."

He ran his hand through his hair, his sign of being flustered. "I wouldn't have helped if you hadn't called. My father was aware of the situation and that it was a demon before others did. I didn't really care either way until you called me." He sounded so guilty.

Laughter bubbled out for the first time in days and burst out of me like a dam breaking loose. I laughed so hard my side started to ache at the strain and I had to clutch my sides.

Shax stared at me like I had lost my mind and that just made me laugh harder. Soon, his shoulders were shaking and snickers and snorts were coming from his mouth before he laughed too. We laughed together for the first time in a long time and it felt almost like being home again.

"Shax," after a few minutes I was able to get out the words, "I don't blame you. It wasn't your problem, even if you were aware of it. You weren't welcome here for a long time. What matters is that you came when asked. You didn't even hesitate even though the last time you were here my Uncle threatened to kill you and Akira punched you." I placed a hand on his knee closest to me and squeezed it. "Thank you."

His hand covered mine and he started down at them. "I missed this." His voice was soft. "You. I've missed your laugh."

I pulled away gently. "Shax," I tried to soften my words, "I love Akira and Lucien. I've missed our friendship, though." Lies upon truths.

His eyes met mine and they were determined. "I'll accept friend-ship. For now." He smirked. "But I should let you know. I'm moving back to Arizona. So, I'm not giving up." He pressed his lips to mine so quickly and pulled back that I wasn't even sure he'd kissed me.

Oh, boy.

I left Shax in his room and went back to mine shortly after he announced that he was going to try to win me back. I rubbed my arms as I walked back into my temporary room. Akira and Lucien were already back and sitting on the bed. They engulfed the bed to where it almost looked like a toddler bed by their size.

Lucien had his head on Akira's shoulder and their hands were clasped together in comfort. They both smiled as I came into the room and closed the door. I stood there for a few seconds, not sure what to do.

They held out their free arms and I was pulled across both of their laps. I sat in Akira's lap with my legs draped over Lucien's, it was comforting and familiar. Akira wrapped his arm around my waist tightly and he and Lucien's clasped hands rested in my lap. Lucien held my legs close to him.

"I thought I had lost you. I can't go through that again." I looked up at Akira.

"I'm sorry, baby. I thought you were told that I was alright. Seems like there is a serious miscommunication issue with the healers and MEPA." Akira grumbled softly as his lips grazed my forehead.

Lucien squeezed my legs and stroked my calf. "I'll talk with the head healer. I'm sorry, love. But we're together now, I shouldn't have let your Uncle push me out before." So that's why there had been the sound of a scuffle as they left the room. Uncle Ray had literally dragged Lucien away. I'd need to have a talk with him.

We held each other for a long time after that. We were still holding each other when a healer came into the room about twenty minutes later. She didn't even blink at the three of us basically pretzeled together on the tiny bed. She did push the men out of room to do a final exam.

"Can I go home?" After she finished, I pulled on my clothes again.

"I believe so. You're still going to be sore for a few more days, so no **strenuous** activity. Your lung is healed but it's still vulnerable to strain and that could land you back in here." She empathized. "If you can promise that, I'll release you to your men with instructions on your care."

Amusement glinted in my eyes as she let them back into the room and told them the news that we basically wouldn't be able to have sex for a few more days. Akira groaned dramatically and Lucien grinned at me as they both promised to make sure to behave. It didn't take long to get my things that Uncle Ray brought me and out to the parking lot.

Akira led us to a brand new white truck and I raised an eyebrow. He shrugged and placed the items in the bed of the truck and the balloons and flowers into the back of the truck.

"You didn't expect me to drive a car, did you?" He didn't let me climb into the truck, he just lifted me to the middle as Lucien buckled up in the passenger side.

Lucien wrapped his arm around my shoulders and I placed a hand on Akira's thigh. "I love you both. Can we go home now?"

"I thought you'd never ask." Akira grinned as the truck turned on and he kissed me roughly. Lucien was right behind him as Akira's lips left mine, Lucien's were claiming mine. I shivered and my hand clenched on Akira's thigh.

"Why do we have to wait again?" I was breathless by the time Lucien let me up for air.

"No cheating." Lucien kissed me again gently. "But I think Akira and I can give you a show to enjoy, hmm?"

"Hell, yes." Akira pressed down on the gas as we left the medical ward parking lot. The building was just as non-descript as Lucien's office. "We're going to Lucien's tonight, but tomorrow we'll head out to my place. After that? We'll figure it out together."

"Where ever you guys are is home." The future wasn't something I used to really care about but now it seemed to be filled with hope. With them at my side I could take on anything.

To be continued......

Take heart, The Panda Over Lords have arrived for our salvation.

GHOST TRANCE: REVENGE OF THE SNOWMAN

A SHORT GHOST DUD STORY

"Vic," Uncle Ray rumbled from his side of the bar, "how come no one told me that shaman could outdrink even me?" His miserable voice was muffled in his arms. "He even outdrank that damn red haired demon."

"It's not my fault you decided to challenge Shane when he was channeling Spirit." I hummed happily as I was cleaning up the empty glasses that littered the bar. "How much did you lose?"

Uncle Ray groaned, as if in pain. "Over five hundred dollars. That bald bastard played me." He growled the last part but whimpered as he pulled his head up. He looked green, even his signature mustache looked lifeless.

My chuckle was soft. Shane had come in with his family to celebrate his son, Trey's, ninth birthday. I had thought he was too old for such young kids but it turns out he and his wife ended up adopting after their biological kids reached adulthood.

Even though we were a bar, I owed Shane for the help he'd given me over the last couple of months. When he'd called me asking for my opinion on where they could have a surprise party, I'd instantly suggested Sups Karaoke Bar. Shane had said they didn't have a big budget so the bar was the perfect place to have it. The kid's birthday was on a Monday, so we would normally not be busy. It wasn't hard to convince Uncle Ray to shut down the bar for the night.

When the pack had heard we were closed because it was for a kid's birthday party, most of them came to help set up the party. They had all brought presents for each of the kids as well. Shifters had a thing for kids; the whole protective instinct thing.

Shane's wife, Lucile, hadn't expected everyone to pitch in. She was teary eyed through most of the party while the kids played around with some of the shifters in their wolf forms.

It was only after the presents had been opened that Uncle Ray had challenged Shane to a drinking contest. He'd bet that if he'd won, Shane would have to bless the bar for prosperity. I was pretty sure Shane would have done it if he'd just asked. What Uncle Ray hadn't anticipated was Spirit, the elemental, joining in through Shane.

"You can let Chase finish cleaning up, Vic." He grabbed a glass of water, sipping it. "He's due back in a minute. Why not say goodbye to your friends before they leave?"

"Thanks, Uncle Ray." Usually, I'd insist on finishing what I'd started but I did want to say goodbye to Shane and his family.

They were in the parking lot behind the bar. Shane was putting the piles of presents into the back of their van. The weather didn't seem to faze him. The nights were getting cold now that we were approaching winter. Shane was an older man with a shaved head. All of his hair was in his massive beard.

"Shane! Did Trey have a good birthday?" Grabbing a few of the smaller packages, I helped put them in the van.

"He and his siblings had a blast. They're all conked out already." He finished putting in the last package. "I wanted to thank you for tonight. When I first called you, I thought the most we would get was a place to have dinner with presents. We didn't expect the pack." His eyes shimmered in the low light with tears as he stroked his long beard. "Even that drinking contest was fun. Spirit hasn't come out just for fun in a very long time."

Laughing, I hugged Shane. "Uncle Ray had a blast. No one's beaten him at drinking in a long time. I have to thank you both for taking him down a peg. I know Lucien wanted to be here but he got called away on some new case. Akira said to tell you hello too. He's flying back from visiting his family in Texas but he won't be back until tomorrow morning."

"Ah, I know Lucile was curious where those two were."

We walked to the driver's side of the van. When I looked in the windows, his whole family was asleep.

"Trey had said he wanted to play in snow for his birthday, but being in Gilbert at this time of year made that pretty much impossible. He came to us from a bad situation, our goal was to give him whatever he wanted but there's been no snow in Flagstaff yet, either." Shane's voice was soft but filled with love. "The packs gifts more than made up for the lack of snow, I think."

"You guys are always welcome to come to the bar. As you saw, the pack adores your kids." I snickered softly. "Plus, seeing your little ones riding on the back of some of the wolves? That's given me blackmail material that'll last for months."

Shane let out his belly laugh, forgetting he was trying to be quiet. "You're welcome?" He shook his head. "You have a good night. Tell your Uncle that I'll come to collect my money later." He winked as he opened his driver's side door, sliding into the car. "I already did a blessing before leaving, but don't tell him."

As they pulled out of the parking lot, a small smile stayed on my lips as I waved goodbye. Tonight had been a good one, it had just been for the sake of a child, but it had also been good for everyone else too. A chill wind wound itself through the parking lot, making my hair move slightly. It was becoming a chilly night, I headed back into the bar to help finish cleaning up.

.⋰ ⋯ ⋱. ⋰ ⋯ ⋱. ⋰ ⋯ ⋱.

Later that morning, just as dawn had started to peak over the horizon, I climbed into Akira's large bed. My guys were out either visiting family or working. It was the first night I was going to be sleeping alone in a long while. Fighting back the feeling of loneliness, I stretched under the warm comforter. They'd be back in the morning so I had to suck it up. After exchanging a few texts with my men, I settled in to sleep.

It felt like I had literally just closed my eyes when my ringtone went off. My hands slapped out to shut it off when my hand hit solid flesh.

"What?" My hand moved upward to a chin before it was caught in a warm grip.

"Feeling frisky this early in the morning?" The gruff voice purred in my ear. My eyes flew open to meet those of Shax. "Good morning, my sweet." His skin was warm against mine.

"What... when?" My mouth felt like it was stuffed with cotton.

Shax was naked to the waist. My eyes wandered over the planes of his chest, drinking in the muscles. His trademark smirk caused shivers to move through my body. My fingers were already running through his short dark red hair.

"The other two are in the kitchen. I was tasked with waking you up. There's a surprise outside we think you're going to like." He leaned forward, brushing his lips against my neck. "Or we could stay in bed all day." I watched as his eyes flashed a deeper green from his usual light green.

My head was fuzzy. There was something wrong, I just couldn't put my finger on it. Before I could contemplate the situation, Shax distracted me as he stood out of the bed, stretching with his arms reaching to the ceiling. He confirmed my suspicions that he had no clothes on. The sight of him just that made my pussy throb in need. His back was littered in scars but they just added to his exotic beauty.

He looked over his shoulder at me to wink. "Keep looking at me like that, my sweet, I'll make the decision for you." He chuckled as I scrambled out of bed.

"I'll see you in the dining room!" Not bothering to get dressed, I ran into the living room in my pajama shirt (it was actually Akira's shirt, but it fit like a dress and was more comfortable). "Lucien! Akira!" Seeing both of them at the dining table made my chest warm.

"There she is." Akira grinned as I dived on top of him. He pulled me into his lap, ignoring that I bumped into the table, almost spilling the drinks. "You were sleeping like the dead." Just looking up into his warm smile made me want to purr like a cat. His silver eyes were filled with amusement as his eyes moved down my body. "I see you're wearing my shirt." His black hair that was tipped in red brushed my forehead as he leaned in to kiss me gently.

"Shax said there's a surprise?" I glanced between the two men. I couldn't hold back the smile that spread across my face.

"That idiot didn't give anything away, did he?" Akira growled playfully. "I'll kick his ass if he did."

"As kinky as that sounds, puffball," Shax sauntered into the room wearing loose pants that showed off his impressive chest, "we'll have to wait for that after the surprise. I wouldn't ruin it for her." He chuckled as Akira grumbled at him. Shax kissed the top of my head before sitting in Lucien's lap.

Lucien's lips twitched in amusement as Akira continued to glare at Shax. His hands stroked Shax's sides before he pressed his lips to the side of Shax's neck. "Good morning, babe." He had his chestnut hair in his signature braid over his right shoulder.

My chest pounded in happiness with the three of them here. There was still something strange about this but it was so far from my mind, I didn't care anymore.

"What's the surprise?" Grabbing a piece of toast from Akira's plate, I nibbled on it.

"It's outside. Finish your breakfast, we'll all go out together." Lucien pushed a plate of fruit with another piece of toast at me. "You too, Shax." He picked Shax up like he didn't weigh a thing, placing him in the seat next to him. Lucien picked up his cup of tea, sipping it as he watched us eat, his solemn brown eyes missing nothing.

Akira let me stay in his lap as I finished breakfast. I took advantage of that by wiggling every so often as I felt him harden against my ass. His chest vibrated as he fought a growl while I moved to torture him. He gripped my waist tightly, right on the edge of bruising before he bit down on my neck.

"Ah!" My hands slapped down onto the table at the pleasure that bite sent through my body. "Akira!"

"Turnabout's fair play, love." He grumbled, licking the spot he bit before kissing it gently. "I think they're done with their breakfast."

Shax had barely touched his but he was the first to jump to his feet. "Let's go!" He rushed towards the front door.

"Shax, don't forget a jacket." Lucien called after him as he stood, came over to Akira to swing me up into his arms. "And you, let's get you in shoes and a coat."

"Why do I need a coat? It's only been cold at night." Lucien set me down in front of the coat closet, handing me one of his coats after I pulled on my shoes.

"You'll see." He winks at me as he puts on another of his coats. Akira was right behind him but he just pulled his shoes on. Akira usually ran hot since he was a werewolf.

Akira opened the door as Shax ran outside. Lucien followed behind. I went after but stopped in the doorway as my mouth gaped open like a fish out of water. Instead of the normal desert landscape of dirt with some scattering of cactus or flowers, the world was blanketed in white.

"How?" My voice was soft as I stepped out onto the porch, the snow crunching lightly under my feet. "Snow?"

"Snow!" Akira laughed from behind me before scooping me up in his arms. "No idea how but it's the whole valley."

He set me down next to Lucien as we looked around the white landscape. Shax was on the ground making a snow angel, which was ironic, considering he was part demon. It looked like we had gotten a fair amount of snow too, not just a light dusting. The snow came up above my ankle, we might even get more if the clouds above us were any indication.

"Let me guess. Everything is closed down." Arizonians in the valley could barely drive in the rain properly; I could only imagine the havoc snow would cause.

"You would guess right." Lucien chuckled softly. "It's officially a snow day for us."

"You know what that means?" Akira yelled suddenly right as a ball of snow hit Lucien square in the face with a loud smack. "Snowball fight!"

My mouth dropped before I ended up laughing so hard, I was bent over clutching my stomach. Lucien wiped the snow from his face calmly before he looked over at Akira. He held up his left hand in a fist, his metal prosthetics flashing in the light.

"You understand that this means war now." His voice was mild, like he was just discussing dinner. "I won't go easy on you just because you give good head."

Akira laughed evilly. "Bring it on, Bubble Butt." He was taunting Lucien as he was steadily building himself a pile of perfectly formed snowballs.

"*Ventus!*" Lucien threw his left hand out, his fingers splayed. A gust of wind picked up around him before hurtling towards Akira, snow mixed in with the wind. Akira was buried under a mountain of snow in seconds.

"Psst." Shax motioned over to me from where he lay in the snow. "Let's let the buff guys try to bury each other. Want to build a snowman with me?" That last part was given in a sing song voice that caused me to snort.

"Sure, Anna."

He held out his hand to me. I grabbed it with both of mine, helping him stand without ruining his snow angel. He wrapped an arm around my waist, brushing some hair that had fallen into my face.

"If you get too cold, make sure you tell one of us." He smiled knowing that I was no match for his charm when he did that.

"Alright." I had to act like he didn't affect me though. Otherwise, he'd try to have sex in the snow right here. "A snowman? We don't have any carrots or any of the stuff to make him."

"Nonsense." Shax brushed some snow from his loose pants. His jacket wasn't zipped, his abs flashed the world in all their glory. "We can use those black rocks by the cactuses. We'll use something from Akira's truck. You know he has something we can use in there. For the nose we'll use one of the cucumbers."

"That's going to be one weird looking snowman." But I was already running inside to grab said cucumber as Shax went about grabbing the other things we'd need.

Lucien had managed to somehow magic himself a wall of snow. Akira had gotten out of the pile of snow that had been thrown on him, using the pile to hide behind. He was now throwing his snowballs using his full strength at the wall of snow that protected Lucien. Lucien was kneeling behind the wall, but instead of making snowballs, he was making some kind of ward.

"Stop cheating!" Akira yelled out to him.

"I'm using my assets, Puffball!" He yelled another spell; this one was a whirlwind that took the snow and blinded Akira.

"Your ass has nothing to do with this!"

Shax was across the other side of the yard, already rolling the large parts of the snowman together. He had the bottom done, which was already at his shoulders, with the middle part being rolled as I went back to him. He had to have used his ice magic to make it that large, there wasn't that much snow. At least, I didn't think there was.

"I got the cucumber." There was a small pile of dark rocks next to the bottom part of the snowman, I placed the cucumber next to the pile. It was going to be a weird looking nose.

My hair blew as wind surrounded us briefly. Lucien had used another spell to bury Akira in snow. A small smile curved along my lips as I glanced over at them. Even though they were battling it out, there was glee on their faces.

"Can you see if you can find a scarf in Akira's truck for me, Sweets?" Shax had just finished the middle part of the snowman, having placed it on top of the bottom part. "I'll finish the head."

"Sure." The truck was only a little ways away. It was usually unlocked. Akira's neighbors weren't too far away but there was still plenty of space that if someone approached the house, Akira would sense it immediately. He never locked his truck when we were at his home.

The passenger side door opened after a quick tug. The cold had made the doors stick together. Akira threw extra clothing in the backseat just in case he ended up shifting somewhere that he didn't have time to take his clothes off and he ended up shredding his clothes. There had to be a scarf in here somewhere. Maybe.

After a few minutes of digging around, I gave up. Why would a werewolf have a scarf? They were basically their own walking heaters. There was an old gym t-shirt that could work. I would just need to cut off the top of it. It could be more like an ascot but the snowman was already unconventional with its nose.

When I closed the truck door, I noticed that Akira and Lucien were no longer in the middle of their snowball fight. They'd joined Shax at the snowman. It had suddenly gotten larger than it had been before. The middle part of the snowman was at the tip of Akira's head. Lucien was squatting in front of the head with Shax. They both had serious faces as they were working on the face. Shax was holding up the cucumber, but as I watched him, he licked the tip.

He wasn't looking at the face of the snowman though, he was looking over at Akira.

Blinking at him and the ridiculous action, I shook my head. Those two really needed to just sleep with each other. Akira was fine with Shax being in the family, but I knew that he was attracted to him just as much as Shax was attracted to him. They'd yet to touch each other in passion, though. Just heavy glances and the occasional touch.

Lucien pushed Shax's shoulder, bringing his attention back to the snowman's face. Lucien was in love with Shax, too. They'd bonded on our last adventure together. Plus, Lucien was more open with his feelings about him than our angry puffball.

"Hey, big guy," the snow made that crunch noise as I walked over to Akira, "I thought we could use this old t-shirt. We could make it into an ascot for the snowman."

Akira grinned at me, leaning forward to kiss me gently. "Sounds like a plan." He took the shirt from me. He ripped at the arms, separating the top from the middle part of the shirt. No scissors needed.

"Hey, babe," Shax waved to us, "could you place the head on the snowman?" He'd asked Akira. My mouth fought its smile at Akira's reaction.

Akira was tense as his cheeks darkened, but I could tell that he was pleased with being called that by Shax. He just wouldn't say it.

"Don't call me that." Akira grumbled good naturedly, but walked over to the head of the snowman. He didn't look at the face as he picked it up, he just brought it over to the body. He had to stand on his toes to finish putting it on top of the body. He took the torn shirt, pressing it into the right side of the snowman's top and middle part. He even fluffed it up, which caused the rest of us to laugh at how thoughtful he was being. He pulled the hat he was wearing off his head before plopping it on top of the snowman's head.

We all stepped back together to admire it. The face, that

Lucien and Shax worked on, looked kind of like a pirate. One eye was huge, while the other was much smaller. The nose consisted of the cucumber half buried in its face. It looked like they'd used prickly pear fruit instead of rocks for the mouth. With the added ascot, the snowman looked absolutely ridiculous. Shax had sculpted some arms that ended in claws with his ice powers.

"I think we should name him." Shax stood with his feet spread. "What does everyone think of Lucy?"

Lucien snorted softly before his arm wrapped around Shax's shoulders. "I second that."

Akira groaned but just shook his head. "It was your idea, so we'll name the damn thing Lucy."

They all looked at me to make sure I agreed. My laughter was their answer.

"Fine, Lucy it is." Shax looked proud of himself as we all looked at the snowman named Lucy. "Maybe we should give him a mustache? We could cut up a green pepper."

"You already used one of the cucumbers, we aren't using any more of the food. Besides, the green pepper is going to be used for tonight's stir fry." Akira grumbled as he shook his head.

"Ah, well. I don't want to mess up your dinner feng shui. You happen to be the best cook out of all of us." Shax shrugged his shoulders as he looked at Lucy. He missed the pleased look on Akira's face before he turned away.

"You know what snow calls for?" Thinking it was time to distract them, I stepped toward Lucy before spinning to face them. "I think we should make some hot cocoa with chili powder. We could find a board game to play?" The more I thought about it, the more I wanted to relax with my men and just enjoy the snow day.

.· ··· ˙·. .·˙ ··· ˙·. .·˙ ··· ˙·.

A few hours later, we were lounging in the living room. We'd turned on Netflix to their 24 hour fireplace channel that they usually had going for Christmas. We'd finished dinner and now were all spread out on the floor around the board game. Akira had pulled out 'Trouble' from the closet.

"Why did you get to be red, again?" Shax teased me. He was laying on his side with the side of his head propped on his hand directly across from me.

"Because I'm the only one here with a vagina?" I pressed the dome in the middle of the board to roll the dice.

"It is a nice one." Shax wiggled his eyebrows at me as I rolled my eyes in response.

Lucien was lounging on my left side, his hand ran along my calves making me shiver, as well as distracting me from the game. Akira was on my right. He'd started running his hand along my arm that I was using as a pillow.

"Distracting me won't help you guys win." Shooting both of them glares, my last piece landed on top of Akira's last one, sending it back to the beginning. He growled as I laughed evilly. Usually Akira won any video game we played but he sucked at board games.

"No, distracting you is just fun." Lucien's voice pulled my attention from Akira. His fingers brushed behind my right knee, which made a shiver of pleasure roll right up between my legs. "What does the winner get?" His warm eyes pulled me in, the gold around his irises never ceased to make me melt.

"Um," my brain short circuited as his fingers started moving upwards, "sex?"

Three male chuckles surrounded me.

"That means everybody wins." Lucien raised an eyebrow at me.

Clearing my throat, I thought about what I would want if I won.

"Ok, whoever wins, gets to give one command that has to be followed. No matter what."

That seemed to get their attention. Akira cursed again. There was no way he'd be able to catch up but the other two were only a few spaces behind mine but with two more pieces. I only had one left.

"Done." Lucien pressed the dome, getting to move forward three spaces.

"Oo, I want to win!" Shax flashed a grin at me as his eyes roamed the length of my body. He was only able to move one space after he'd pressed the dome.

"Over my dead body!" Akira pressed the dome but groaned when he rolled a five. He had to have rolled a six to continue from the beginning again. Being competitive wasn't helping him in this game.

It was my turn again. I had two spaces to go. The odds were in my favor. Pressing down the dome, I watched the guys reactions instead of the dice. Their combined groans meant I won. Laughing I moved my last piece.

"I win!" Triumphantly, I stood up. "Now, to my command."

Three sets of suspicious eyes looked up at me. I grinned down at all three of them.

"Akira," looking at him, I pointed towards Shax, "make out with Shax until I say you can stop."

"What?!" He jolted up to his feet.

Shax looked between us, his facial expression was concerned and wary, not at all normal for my demon. He liked Akira but I knew Akira's weariness concerned him.

"You agreed to it. That's my command."

"She's right, Akira." Lucien stood, packing up the game. "You agreed." He put the game under his arm that he'd packed up as he helped Shax stand. He noticed Shax's apprehension so he stroked Shax's cheek gently.

"Fine!" Akira stomped over to Shax. He was a few inches taller than him. Akira grabbed Shax's shirt, yanking him forward, away from Lucien, as he crashed his lips to Shax's.

Shax looked like he couldn't believe what was happening. I noticed he was already hard even before his hands had a chance to clutch Akira's shirt tightly. I couldn't believe Akira had actually done it. Shax wrapped his arms around Akira's neck as Akira started to stroke his hands down Shax's body.

Akira started rubbing Shax's nipples roughly with his thumbs creating a much more erotic whimper from Shax than I was expecting. There were moments when I could see their tongues intertwining between their lips and the heat between them was in turn growing between my thighs. This was so much hotter than I could have imagined.

I looked at Lucien who was watching in stunned silence, his jaw slack. I looked down as I saw a twitching in his pants from the corner of my eye. I licked my lips and before I knew it, I had leaned forward and was undoing Lucien's pants. He was so entranced by the scene before him that he hadn't noticed my actions until his cock was encased in my mouth. He hissed from the sudden pleasure and looked down at me with a wicked grin.

"Nn...such a naughty girl." He stroked his large hand over my hair before it slid under the front of my collar. He easily found my breast and pinched and rolled my nipple between his fingers drawing a moan out of me. I started bobbing my head, taking his cock almost to the hilt. He laid his head back moaning in ecstasy, but soon he gently lifted my head. His breathing was labored as he looked down at me with flames in his eyes.

"I won't last long if you keep that up." Like the gentleman he was he grabbed one of the heavy jackets and made a small bed for my back before he laid me back. He grinned sending shudders through every fiber of my being. He knew what that smile did to me. I pulled my arms up and over my head giving him full permission to have his way with me. That seemed to strike his fancy as he quickly spread my legs revealing my already soaked mound. A growl escaped his lips before he clutched my hips. My hips jerked up in anticipation and my mind became fuzzy at the sensation of his perfect cock sliding deep within me.

As he began thrusting, I arched my chest into his and his lips trailed along my neck before he nibbled on my collarbone. That sent my head reeling. My pussy clenched tightly around his cock making him moan as his hips slapped rapidly against mine. I twined my fingers through his luscious hair as our heavy breathing created a cloud of heat around our bodies. When he suddenly bit down on my collarbone a wave of ecstasy overcame me as I reached my climax. My body shuddered and spasmed from the intense orgasm and his soon followed. I felt his hot cum fill me to the brim and his cock twitched wildly inside of me. I clutched his body against mine as my body writhed from the intense pleasure. We lay panting on the floor in a sated daze.

I let me eyes wander to the scene that had riled us up so immensely and my eyes widened. Akira was clutching Shax's ass so tightly I could see the bulges of flesh from below his pants. Shax was panting like a dog through their still intense makeout session as their hips were gyrating together. They were dry humping each other like there was no tomorrow and I could tell they were both close to climax. Shax clenched Akira's shirt in his fists before I saw his body shudder from here. It was so erotic seeing them go at each other like that.

Akira followed suit and a growl rumbled from his throat as he slammed their hips together one more time drawing a whimper from Shax. Akira threw his head back and the dark stain that formed in both of their pants solidified what had happened. They both came in spectacular fashion before leaning against each other to keep from falling over. Their hot panting was all that could be heard now.

"That" when I started talking it seemed to jar them from their bubble of ecstasy, "was so incredibly hot."

Akira was stunned by what just happened, but soon he was grinning down at Shax who was still in a daze. Something told me this wasn't the end of the experimenting. When I glanced over at Lucien my suspicions were proven correct. He was already spreading my legs for another round.

.·˙···˙·.˙···˙·.˙···˙.

It was close to one in the morning according to the clock on the side of the bed. I was laying across Lucien's chest, trailing a finger along his right pec. Akira was sleeping with Shax curled around him. They'd worn each other out and hadn't even had sex yet. Lucien had done so many things with his mouth that had my legs still shaking. His mouth had to be some kind of secret weapon. My family had grown over the past few months and my heart hadn't been so filled in years.

"Aren't you tired, baby?" His voice rumbled softly.

"Sorry, I thought you were asleep." I kept my voice quiet so we didn't wake up the other two. "I was just thinking about how lucky I am."

"Oh?" His left hand moved, stroking the curve of my ass, his metal prosthetic fingers cool against my skin. "I'd say we're the lucky ones."

Suppressing the shudder of pleasure at his touch, I rested my chin on his chest, looking at him. "Lucien, do you think we could go on a holiday vacation, all of us, come Christmas?"

His eyes softened. "I can get the time off. I'm sure my boss won't mind. I bet the guys won't have a problem either." He leaned his head forward, kissing my nose. "Now, let's try to get some sleep, alright?"

A large yawn was his answer as my body drifted into a dream state. My eyes were closed and I could feel myself about to drift off when, just as suddenly, a loud thump noise sounded from outside. The ground shook as if there was an earthquake for a second.

I yanked myself up into a sitting position as another loud thump boomed outside. The guys all sat up looking around as confused as I was.

"What the heck?" Akira grumbled just as the ground shook again, this time followed up with the sound of breaking glass and an alarm from his truck. "My truck!" Akira scrambled out of the bed, pulling on a pair of sweats as he ran out the bedroom door.

"Wait for us!" Lucien called after Akira, he didn't bother with clothes, rushing after him.

"Come on, love." Shax seemed to be the calmest of the three. He rolled out of bed, already dressed in pajama bottoms. He grabbed a robe, tossing it to me. "Let's see what's messing with our puffball's truck."

I stood, putting on the robe, tightening the rope so that I was sufficiently covered. Shax held out some tennis shoes, even though I usually wore sandals, but with the snow, tennis shoes were smart. The front door was wide open when we reached it.   A deafening roar shattered into the air. Clapping my hands over my ears, we both rushed outside.

"No flipping way." Shax was next to me as we both stared in shock at the scene before us.

What was in front of us took several seconds to process. Akira's truck was torn into literal pieces, it was scattered around the yard. The thing that was causing the mass of destruction was none other than Lucy.

Besides the fact that Lucy, the snowman, was alive, it'd grown at least five times bigger. When the prickly pear fruit had looked funny on it earlier today, now the fruit had formed together in a mouth that looked like it had sharp teeth with blood all over them.

The ice arms with claws were now causing damage as it swiped its right arm at Akira who was attempting to use his half formed claws from his wolf on the lower part of Lucy. That just seemed to just piss it off more. It glided along the ground as it moved to try to hurt my men.

Lucien was on the other side of Lucy, completely naked. He knelt on his right knee, his left hand was pressed into the ground, we could see bright blue light emanating from the ground, he'd cast a ward spell but it must be taking its time to activate.

"I've cast a look away spell. No one should be able to see what's happening." Lucien yelled over the roars of Lucy. "But it's not going to last long!"

"Stay back, Vic." Shax ran towards Akira, forming an ice shard before throwing it like a javelin. The ice shard sunk into the middle part of Lucy.

Lucy glanced down as Shax threw more ice shards into its middle. Lucy threw its head back as it roared. The ice shards sunk into its middle and disappeared. Shax cursed as Lucy's other arm slashed downward. He dove to the side, barely missing the claw. He scrambled over to Lucien. Akira had moved around Lucy as well, joining them.

I glanced around. There had to be something I could do. My clairvoyance magic was not going to be of any help here. My eyes were searching the yard when they landed on the water hose. Maybe that could work.

"*Ignis!*" Lucien slammed his right hand onto the ward. It flared to life, turning from blue to a dark red. Flames shoot upward before curving to slam into the monstrous snowman.

Lucy threw up its arms in an x to protect itself from the fire. I didn't understand why they didn't melt, they were made of ice, but the fire dissipated after several seconds. Lucien ran to the left of Lucy with the other two, getting behind the torn bed of Akira's truck.

Shax formed a large shard of ice in his hands, throwing it over the truck bed. It just pissed Lucy off. "Well, that didn't work." Shax sounded nonchalant as the monstrous snowman roared in its rage.

I didn't understand why he didn't try using his earth magic instead.

"No, shit! Why did you think that would work on a SNOW-MAN?" Akira growled from next to him. I was about to snap at him for being mean to Shax.

Shax just laughed and in the middle of dodging the tip of the Lucy claws, he planted a loud kiss right on Akira's lips.

"Oh, angry puffball, no faith!" He dodged the halfhearted swipe from Akira's sharp claws that he'd formed from his half form. "I'll take this thing down, and when I do, I want a repeat from earlier!"

Lucy threw its claws downward. The men had to throw themselves to the ground to get away from it.

Alright, enough of this. I raced around the porch to the water hose. Turning on the spigot to full blast, I aimed it at the back of Lucy, at the bottom of it.

"What are you doing, Vic?" Shax yelled at me from twenty feet away.

He stomped on the ground; a large piece of the ground flew up into the air. He threw his arm making the rock smash into Lucy. That seemed to make the monstrous snowman pause briefly. Akira took advantage of its distraction as he threw his arms into the snow, using his claws to help him start climbing up it.

"Babe," Lucien was next to me, still naked as the day he was born, "What are you doing?" He kept his voice low, making sure not to get Lucy's attention. I was worried that he was going to hurt his feet out in the snow. Not to mention he was naked and it was distracting because I wanted to jump him.

"Lucy won't be able to move if it's slush, right?" Even as we spoke, we could start to see a slow reaction to the water on Lucy's back that was mixing with its snow. It wasn't making much of a difference yet but it would the more water was applied.

"You're brilliant!" Lucien kissed me roughly for several moments. The hose clamored to the ground. Lucien pulled back grinning down at me. "You probably just defeated this thing."

He turned towards Lucy before kneeling on the ground, starting to draw another ward into the snow. He kept an eye on Lucy and our other men.

I picked up the hose again, pulling it away from Lucien so that it didn't interfere with his spell. I moved over, still spraying the bottom back part of Lucy. Shax was still dodging its claws, having gotten cut a few times, he was bleeding from his side.

Akira was hanging near the ascot. He was using his strength to bury into Lucy's neck with his right claw, trying to rip its head off. Lucy grabbed at him, throwing him down onto the ground. Akira tucked himself as he rolled and hit the ground. Shax was at his side, throwing up an ice shield as Lucy's claws slammed downward.

"Hurry, Lucien!" I angled the hose so that it started hitting water at Lucy's head, trying to get its attention off of the other two.

Just as Lucy turned toward me, slower than it had been since the bottom back of its body was now starting to turn to slush, Lucien cried out his spell.

"*Aqua urna Ventus!*" As he shouted his spell, wind rushed at Lucy, carrying with it, a stream of water. As Lucien held his arms both out straight, the wind whirled around Lucy and the water stream got stronger.

Lucy began to fall over as its bottom half had turned to slush, sliding left as it tried to go right. It screamed in rage but Lucien's spell soon overwhelmed it. After a few minutes, Lucy was a puddle of slush. The materials that we'd used on Lucy went back to their original size. I picked up the cucumber that had been its nose, looking at it curiously. What had caused this weird situation to happen?

"How in the world did our snowman turn into a raging snow monster?"

Shax, supported by Akira, came over to us as Lucien stood. "That is the question. Why don't we get inside? Lucien, love, you need to get warm before you get frostbite."

Lucien looked down in surprise. "Oh, I forgot."

We all went back inside. It still didn't feel real that there had been a monster snowman attacking us just moments ago. Lucien went straight to the master bathroom, starting a warm bath. Akira had shifted back to his human form as he brought Shax into the bathroom.

Lucien moaned as he got into the bath. Shax stripped slowly, wincing in pain, but Akira was gentle as he helped him into the bath with Lucien. I left the men to it; I knew Lucien would do something to help Shax with his pain. The men soaked in the tub together for twenty minutes before they were warm enough. We all climbed into bed together, pulling the blanket up around us.

Sleep came quickly to all of us. I still felt strange. The last 24 hours was like a dream.

.· ··· ·. .· ··· ·. .· ··· ·.

I grabbed my phone from the bedside table as the ringer went off again. I noticed five missed calls from Shane. Redialing his number, I sat up in bed as my adrenalin started to wear off. My men weren't anywhere to be seen.

"Victoria?" Shane's voice was stressed. "Are you and the men alright?"

"Yes, we're fine. But, uh, well." I paused, not really sure to explain about the snowman. I assumed the guys were ok.

"Oh, thank the gods." Shane took a breath. "Listen, something happened in the last day. Everyone in the pack, including you, have been under a sleep spell. Trey somehow summoned a dream sprite that granted his snow request but it came with a twist."

I rubbed my temples. "What do you mean a sleep spell?"

"It's not as bad as it could have been. Spirit was able to warn me. I've spent the past several hours reversing this spell. The humans are none the wiser, thank the gods. Trey had wanted to repay the packs kindness." He sounded tired. "Whatever happened to you in the past day or so wasn't real."

"So the snowman that turned into a monster and tried to kill us was all a dream?"

"Aye, all a dream." I blew a raspberry. "Can you ask Trey not to make deals with dream sprites without you from now on?"

Shane chuckled. "That's already been talked about. Look, I'll come over tomorrow to check to make sure there are no after residual effects."

"Right. Thanks, Shane." We hung up. I had to shake my head

in wonder. This whole situation had been caused by a kid with a wish.

It had seemed so real. The snowball fight, the board game with the three of them. Even the sex had felt so real.

"Hey babe," Lucien walked into the room, "I just got the text from Shane. Did you have a dream about a snowman too?" He sat on the bed. His hair was mused and falling out of his braid. "Akira had the same dream and I can tell you, he's a little flustered about it." He chuckled at that. "Do you think Shax shared the same dream?"

"It's most likely." I sighed, feeling my face flush. "We all shared it, it seemed."

"I'm not complaining." Lucien laughed softly kissing my hand. "Neither is Akira, even if sharing a dream with Shax unnerved him."

I laughed before picking up my phone again. I flipped open my text messages to see a few from Shax. He had driven back to Las Vegas after the party at the bar. He'd said he'd be gone for a few days at his restaurant. His texts were explicit.

"Yup. He had it too."

"Well, at least we know never to build a snowman together." Lucien helped me out of bed. "Let's go make some food, mm?"

That strange feeling during the dream was now explained. That hadn't been real, but the possibility of it brought a smile to my face as we went into the kitchen to have breakfast with Akira.

The End

OTHER WORKS

Cider Book 9
Secrets of Talonsville Charity Series (%50 of proceeds are donated to charity)
Knight's Talons

Please visit Aspen and her co-author's group on Facebook
Aspen Black and Adammeh's Wanderers

Subscribe to Newsletter

Made in the USA
Las Vegas, NV
06 April 2022

47004611R00121